WHICH WOULD KILL HIM FIRST?

Harrison Ridere wasn't ready to die from the snake bite that clouded his brain—not yet at least. He was drifting in and out of consciousness, struggling to keep awake. He tried focusing on his horse, which was chomping the dry grass a few hundred feet away. If only he could reach it . . .

The effort made his head spin like a toy top and he had to shut his eyes to make it stop. Then there was a sound; the crunch of a footstep on the gravely ground. He listened closer. Was it his imagination? No. He was sure of it now. Somehow, Walter Hodgeback must have trailed him here! Ridere parted his eyelids but the glare of the sun shut them on him. Someone came around the boulder and stopped.

Ridere grabbed for his gun.

The clatter of a Winchester's lever being cycled stopped his hand.

OUTCASTS
BLACK JUSTICE

JASON ELDER

LEISURE BOOKS NEW YORK CITY

A LEISURE BOOK®

July 2000

Published by

Dorchester Publishing Co., Inc.
276 Fifth Avenue
New York, NY 10001

ISBN 0-8439-4744-6

BLACK JUSTICE

Chapter One

Mariposa Springs, a dusty little village at the foot of the San Juan Mountains, sunned itself beneath a Colorado noonday sun. A few men and a couple of horses gathered in the shade of a huge cottonwood tree near the cupola-covered spring on the north end of town. A half dozen or so folks strolled along the boardwalks—women mostly this time of day, doing their shopping or chatting amiably in front of plate-glass storefront display windows.

Other men gathered in the cantina. Life was easygoing in Mariposa Springs, especially on a warm midsummer afternoon, when life slowed to a crawl. It seemed a perfect place for the Outcasts to spend a few days, spend some money, douse the trail dust from their throats.

Dougal O'Brian had headed straight for the Broken Bow Saloon and staked a claim to a spot at the long bar, while Royden Louvel had settled down in an alcove just off the small hotel's lobby. He had rustled himself up a game of cards almost as fast as O'Brian had fetched himself that first beer. A one-armed gambler seemed something of a novelty in Mariposa Springs, and some men figured Louvel an easy mark. Of course, some men have been known to try and outrun locomotives on horseback, too.

John Russell Keane had managed to find his way into the office of the Montezuma County *Messenger*, where Flannigan Claghorn turned out to be a congenial host and showed him to a desk and let him have access to every back issue of the newspaper for the last five months. Keane had been out of touch with news of the country ever since he and Louvel had left Denver City and ridden south to meet up with the others in Gallup, New Mexico Territory.

He was curious to learn how General Miles was handling the Apache problem down along the Mexican border, and if he was having any better luck capturing Geronimo than General Crook had before him. He wanted word on troop movements from Fort Bowie, too. Although that part of his life was long put to rest, he'd yet to be able to bury it completely. Curiosity remained. The army had tainted him in a peculiar way and there seemed little he could do to completely rid himself of that infection.

Nantaje, the ex-Apache scout, was always uncomfortable in a village full of white men, and he generally tagged close to either Keane or Louvel. At the moment he was sitting out behind the newspaper office, turning a perfectly good length of cottonwood into useless slivers with his scalping knife.

And Harrison Ridere? Well, Harrison Ridere was doing what Harrison Ridere always did best. . . .

After an hour wrestling each other in the mad fury of

lovemaking, Harry was exhausted. Exhausted? Was this a first for him? Was he getting old? He worried about it some as Carla Hodgeback nestled down into his arms, her chin resting on his chest, her lanky, naked body pressed hard against his, legs and arms still entangled. Harry wanted to close his eyes and go to sleep, but he resisted the urge, preferring instead to admire the woman in his arms. Carla Hodgeback was beautiful, and a complete stranger to him only two hours earlier.

Harry struggled back a grin. He might be slowing down some, but he had sure been refining his skills. Carla had been a snap to talk to and cajole into his bed—*her* bed. Her bed, her house, her whiskey. He owed some of his good luck, he knew, to Dougal O'Brian's careful coaching. Though an old man now, O'Brian was a true master where the females were concerned. A real Casanova!

Carla moaned softly, contentedly, then kissed him on the earlobe and wiggled out of his arms. Harry sat up, his naked back sticky against the white-washed wall. Carla slipped into her chemise, then straddled a chair, an arm folded across its cane back, her sweaty chin propped on it, her big brown eyes watching him.

"I'm going to get dressed now, Harry," she said with a sigh, standing.

"Sure you don't want to come back for more?" he asked, and patted the crumpled sheet.

Carla laughed. "You done me all in, Harry. And I'm not in the mood no more," she added lightly, lifting a limp curl of auburn hair from her forehead and frowning at herself in the mirror.

Ridere reached for the bottle on the bedstand. He should be drinking water instead of whiskey in this heat, but whiskey was all Carla said she had in the house.

"Maybe later, after it cools some," he said.

"Maybe."

He looked over suddenly, giving her a suspicious frown. "You are sure your husband's going to be gone all day?"

She laughed lightly. "That's what he said. Rode over to Carson Junction on business day before yesterday. Whenever he does that he don't ever come back right away," she said, prodding hair. "He'll be away a couple more days."

"He goes to Carson Junction often?"

"Once or twice a month."

"What kind of business is he in? You never did get around to saying."

She looked over her shoulder and smiled at him. "You never gave me a chance. Your hands were all over me like flies on sticky paper."

Ridere laughed. "You weren't exactly fighting me off. What's going to happen when words gets back to him?"

Carla shrugged and began pinning her tousled hair back in place. "Walter knows I fool around, though he might get real mad if anyone points it out to him. He'll get over it."

"So, what *does* he do?" Ridere tipped back the bottle and took a drink.

"Walter? Walter is sheriff hereabouts."

Ridere almost choked. He slammed the bottle down and stared at Carla Hodgeback. "Sheriff!"

"Don't worry, honey. Nobody here will talk. Walter would kill anyone who let on that they knew." She grinned. "Walter thinks he's the only one who knows.

He slaps me around some, then feels real bad and comes crawling back."

Ridere swallowed hard and grabbed his shirt, shoving an arm into the sleeve.

"Are you going already?" she inquired.

"Think I better."

"And tonight?"

"Ah . . . ? Better not." He pulled on his trousers and boots and stood. "Maybe some other time."

Carla laughed.

They both heard it just then. "What's that?" he asked, staring at the door behind which he knew was a hallway.

"Sounds like someone come into the parlor," Carla whispered.

"Carla? Carla, honey, you home?"

She stared at him, eyes impossibly wide. "It's Walter!"

"Walter! I thought you said he wasn't going to be back for days!"

"Quick, the window!"

"You in the bedroom, Carla?" the voice said, growing louder down the hallway, and then the doorknob turned.

Ridere grabbed his hat and gunbelt and tried to fold himself through the open window. He got stuck there for a moment. Struggling, his foot kicked the table, knocking the whiskey bottle to the floor.

"Carla? What's going on in there, Carla?"

Harry heard the door open and a man's voice roar behind him. "What's this? Not again, Carla!"

Then Ridere was through the window. He tumbled to the ground and sprang to his feet as a scowling face thrust itself past the light chintz curtains.

"Walter, don't!" Ridere heard Carla cry, near panic.

But he didn't take the time to look back. Ducking his head, he flew like the wind out onto the street. A gunshot rang out and dust kicked up to his right. He ran a zigzagging course and dove through the batwing doors of the cantina.

"Harry?" Dougal O'Brian said, surprised at his explosive entrance. O'Brian was somewhere in his mid-sixties, a veteran of the Mexican American war—on the Mexican side. A San Patricio, and beneath his shaggy, gray beard he carried the branded *D* of a deserter on his cheek to prove it. At the moment O'Brian was supporting himself at the end of the bar, drinking alone. That didn't surprise Ridere. O'Brian liked drinking alone, and at the moment he appeared to be three sheets to the wind. That didn't surprise Ridere either. Ever since they left Father Leandro in Sonoyta and started for California, O'Brian had been sampling the wares of every saloon and cantina along the way. California still looked a long way off at the rate they were going.

"Got trouble a'coming, Dougal!"

"Skirt trouble?" O'Brian slurred.

"Husband trouble!"

A low chuckle rolled through the cantina. "There is a back door, mister," the bartender said.

Ridere rushed through the barroom and out onto the street behind. He hesitated an instant, then dashed to the left and turned up an alley. He drew up at the corner of the building. Across the way he saw a heavy-set man step from Carla's house. He was heading for the cantina, a revolver in his fist, the look of revenge shaping his face. Ridere hunkered down behind an empty rain barrel and waited until Walter Hodgeback had stalked into the cantina, then he sprinted across the street to where his horse chased flies with a lazy tail in the shade of a building.

"There he is," someone said.

Ridere leaped to his saddle and dug in his heels. Walter burst out of the doorway of the cantina and fired three times as he raced for the edge of town.

John Keane stepped out of the newspaper office just as Ridere flew past. Nantaje appeared at his elbow and they looked at each other. Up the street, Royden Louvel emerged from the hotel in time to see the tail end of Ridere's horse flag itself at the town limits. The one-armed gambler caught Keane's eye, and Keane gave the man a shrug. O'Brian staggered out of the saloon just about then, and the three Outcasts converged upon him. If anyone knew what kind of trouble Ridere had gotten himself into this time, Dougal O'Brian would.

Ridere left Mariposa Springs behind and kept his horse to a run for a mile or more before the animal began to lather and he turned off and found a way into some sandstone boulders.

He worked his way to a place where he could watch the road, squinting against the burning sun that glared off the rocks and sear grass that stretched off to the hazy sawtooth range rising in the distance. Walter Hodgeback wasn't long in coming. He rode an easy gait, studying the edge of the road for signs. He stopped a couple of times and squatted there frowning, but he missed the place Ridere had turned off and went past.

Ridere let out a long sigh. That was a close one. Too close. He'd been having a few of them calls lately and he wondered briefly if it wasn't time to quit his dallying—or at least rein it in some. Royden Louvel had warned him about it. O'Brian had already saved him once from an irate father. How long could his luck hold out?

"Maybe forever!" Ridere grinned to himself.

He gave Hodgeback a good fifteen minutes, then scooted down the face of the boulder and started for the place his horse was hidden. He'd have to get word to O'Brian and the others somehow. He had no intentions of going back and telling them himself.

Kicking through the tufts of brittle-dry grass, he caught a streak of movement out of the corner of his eye. Instinctively he leaped to one side, but he was too slow. The rattlesnake was big and fast, and its fangs plunged deep into his calf like two fiery needles. He wheeled around, kicked free of the snake and drew his gun and fired. The snake writhed upon the ground, dead with half its head shot away, but his body didn't know it yet.

Ridere staggered back, clutching the burning spot on his leg, and dropped to the ground, watching the snake slowly settle down until there was nothing left in it but an occasional quiver. A wave of nausea swept over him.

He pushed himself up and started for his horse but fell against one of the rocks. He'd known men who had been snakebit. They seemed all right at first, before slowly sinking into a stupor. But what Ridere felt was a sudden wave of dizziness. Why was it different with him? His head was spinning and he tried to straighten up. Was it the heat? The whiskey he had drunk? He staggered a step for his horse and grabbed for the saddle. The animal danced warily out of his reach, snorting at him and rolling its big eyes. Ridere slumped in a patch of shade. His vision blurred and his leg ached fiercely. Mustering his strength, he tried for the horse again, only driving it farther away.

All he could do was sit there and squeeze his eyes against the fire in his leg and the unrelenting ball of fire that burned in the sky. He rested his head back against a rock, waiting for the spell to pass. But it didn't, and he wondered if this was what it felt like to die.

Chapter Two

When Egan Driscoll stepped into the bunkhouse it was as if an unspoken command for quiet had been given. The amiable murmur went instantly silent. The five men there watched the tall foreman of the Lazy J filling the doorway, glancing around the place, unsmiling, his face hard as Indian flint.

"Casey."

A wrangler sitting on one of the bunks glanced up from the saddlebag he was mending with a big stitching needle and waxed thread. "Mr. Driscoll?"

"I thought I told you to bring in those mustangs from Lionel."

Casey Owen was a tall, narrow-hipped wrangler with a sunburned face and quick blue-gray eyes always on the alert. He was a normally reserved man, and a top hand. Casey had been with John Jacob almost from that first day when the owner of the Lazy J had come into the territory. As far as he was concerned, Egan Driscoll was a newcomer, an interloper. Casey always figured it should have been he who was made foreman, not Driscoll. He didn't completely under-stand why Driscoll got the job instead of himself, but he had his suspicions, and because of that he was care-ful not to ask. Casey was not a man who pried into the affairs of others. Just the same, it was a bitter pill he carried around with him, though he never mentioned it to anyone.

"Me and Peter rode on over to his place this morn-ing. Lionel wasn't there. You know how Lionel can be sometimes. If you took away the wrong mustangs he'd have a fit."

Driscoll's view shifted from Owen to Peter Blake. Blake was not quite twenty; a slightly built, gangly boy who hardly spoke unless spoken to first. He was often-times given to blushing, which put him at the mercy of the harder men . . . especially Egan Driscoll.

"So you two rode clear over to his place, didn't find him at home and just came back. Is that right, Blake?"

"Err . . . yes, sir."

"Did you ever think of waiting there till he came back?"

Blake glanced at Casey, a silent plea for help in his pale blue eyes.

"I . . . suppose maybe we should have waited . . . I guess."

"You guess! What have you got in that head of yours for brains, boy?" His voice turned from rage to mock-ery. "You could have watched all them pretty birdies down along the crik there. You like birdies, don't you, Blake? I've seen you and the boss's daughter together feeding those critters."

A rush of crimson flooded up Blake's neck and set his smooth cheeks glowing. Driscoll laughed. "Don't think I haven't seen the way you carry on over them like she does. Or is it Rachel Jacob you're really interested in? Got an eye for her, do you?"

"I . . . I . . . no, I don't," he stammered, looking away.

"Leave the kid alone, Egan," Casey said, setting the saddlebag aside and standing. "I made the decision to come back, not Pete."

"Then you made a bad decision, Owen. Keep that up and I'll see to it you are out of a job."

Casey's fists bunched at his sides.

Driscoll saw it and laughed. There were gaps in the grin that creased his sunburned face. Egan Driscoll had seen his share of fights and had come out on the winning end of most of them. "Go on, do it. I know it's what you've wanted to do since I was made foreman. It's what every man who works for the Lazy J wants. Don't think I don't know. Throw that punch. And when I get done wiping the ground with you I'll see that John kicks you off his ranch. Go on, do it, Owen."

Casey got control of his anger and slowly relaxed his fists. "No, I'm gonna stick around here a while longer, Egan. I'm curious to see how you get yours. The bigger the braggart, the louder he cries uncle."

"You'll have a long wait then, and I'm not going to make it an easy one." He glanced at Peter Blake. "Barn needs mucking out. See to it." He cast a final look at Casey, then rounded on his heels and strode out the doorway and across the yard toward the stone house nestled in the shade of two huge mulberry trees.

"I'm just liable to kill that man one of these days," Casey said through clenched teeth.

Blake looked over but didn't say a word.

Corey Lomis, Ralph Weatherby, and Hep Johnson had kept quiet while Egan was there, knowing that keeping silent was the safest course to tread whenever Egan Driscoll was around and on one of his rampages—which was generally all the time.

Now Hep Johnson said, "We'd all like to kill that hombre, Casey. And even Lionel feels the same."

"Probably more so," Weatherby allowed. "Like you said, Casey, Driscoll will get his someday."

Hep gave a short laugh. "And that day can't come too soon for my liking."

Driscoll paused in the shade of the mulberry tree, its thick trunk between himself and the young woman in the yard behind the house. Rachel Jacob was sitting in a chair, holding something on her lap while all around her sparrows and finches pecked at the seeds she'd cast across the ground. The blue jays, braver than the others, hopped along the arm of the chair, snatching bits of suet from her fingers.

At nineteen, Rachel was a plain girl, thin, rangy and fair-skinned. She avoided the shriveling Colorado sun, preferring to be out in the early morning or in the cool of the evening after the sun was low. It was at these times that she would take her horse from the barn and ride off alone. Egan had no idea where she went on her frequent rides, nor did he much care.

Rachel held no attraction for him. It wasn't the age difference so much that mattered to Egan. The girl simply had no spirit, and was hard on the eyes to look at. She had a slightly overlarge nose, and her brown eyes seemed to bulge when she looked at you. Her hair was dark brown, like her mother's, but unlike Felicity Jacob, Rachel kept it pinned up severely at the back of her head, hidden beneath her wide sun bonnet. The girl had none of her mother's fire either. Egan gave a smirk, thinking of Felicity Jacob, of that part of her soul that he suspected even her husband, John Jacob, knew nothing about.

Egan stepped around the tree and the birds scattered before him. "Afternoon, Miss Jacob," he said pleasantly, smiling and touching the brim of his wide hat.

"Oh. Hello, Mr. Driscoll," she said coolly. Like nearly everyone else on the Lazy J, Rachel Jacob didn't like him.

Driscoll knew it, but he didn't care. The ones that counted did like him, and that was the way he intended to keep it, even if it meant being polite to their homely daughter. "What do you have there on your lap?" he asked.

She smiled awkwardly and opened her hand, showing him the little pink ball with a slender black beak and a few scraggly feathers making their first appearance. "It's an oriole, I think. There is a nest up there." She pointed to an overarching branch. "I found this one in the grass. Don't know how it survived the fall, but it doesn't appear hurt."

"Sure is ugly, ain't he? What you going to do with the critter?"

"I suppose I'll get one of the hands to bring over a ladder and put him back in the nest."

"Mamma bird will only kick the squirt out again."

She frowned. "Think so?"

Egan laughed. "It's what I'd do to a misshapen critter like that."

"That isn't even funny, Mr. Driscoll!" She glared at him, and he imagined her eyes popping right out of her homely little face.

20

He laughed again and strolled away. As he came around the corner of the house a woman's voice said, "What was that all about?"

Felicity Jacob was wearing a dark blue dress, and standing against the rock wall of the house where the deep shade and the shadow from the chimney made her hard to see. Her hair hung loose and long, and danced across her slender shoulders. He moved closer and put a hand against the wall, corralling her there in the corner.

"Your kid found herself a baby bird."

Felicity smiled, not the least alarmed by his sudden closeness. "She's got a tender heart."

"Hm? Is that what it is?"

"Rachel is a gentle child, so unlike this land—and some people I know," she added, catching his eye.

"Wouldn't swat a fly if it was sitting right on her"— He caught himself and finished—"pretty little nose." Egan glanced around, then turned back and kissed her hard on the lips. It was a long kiss that slowly worked its way up her cheek and to her earlobe. He felt the urgency rising in his body and wanted more, but she pushed him away.

"Not now . . . not here, you fool!" Felicity said, pushing her long hair back out of her face.

"Then when?"

"Later."

He stood away from her. "All right, later."

"He's in the house," she said, smoothing the material of her dress. "I presume that's why you are here."

"I'll be looking for you tonight." Egan grinned and turned away from her. Then he stopped. Rachel was standing by the tree watching him. How long had she been there? he wondered. How much had she seen?

Quickly Egan averted his eyes from her unsmiling stare and hurried around the front of the house and knocked on the door.

"Come in," came the sharp reply from beyond.

John Jacob was a short, heavy man with a bald head and a dark brown beard neatly shaped and cropped close to the skin. His eyes were blue and his skin dark. Unlike his daughter, John Jacob did not shun the sun. He'd worked hard all his life to get where he was today, but once he had arrived, he had eased back some. He let his success settle down around his belt while others did the legwork for him now. Just the same, John Jacob kept an eagle eye on his holdings. Luckily for Egan Driscoll, he did not oversee the affairs of his wife as closely.

"Egan, it's you. Come on in." The owner of the Lazy J was holding a Winchester rifle. He inclined his head at an open door and Egan followed him into the office. Jacob set the rifle atop his cluttered desk, took down a cleaning rod and a bottle of solvent from the gun rack and said, "What's the word on those mustangs?"

"I sent Owen over to collect them and bring them back, but Lionel wasn't there to turn them over to him, so he came back empty-handed."

John Jacob glanced up from his task. "Empty-handed? He left them? Casey Owen is one of the best hands on this ranch. He knows a green broke from a wild one."

Egan gave a short laugh. "That's what I thought. Owen gave me some song and dance about Lionel having a conniption if he took them without his say-so."

"Lionel's say-so? Lionel works for me, and Owen had my say-so!"

"You know how uppity that nigger gets."

Jacob gave him a narrow look. "Lionel is the best

damned bronc-buster within a hundred miles of here, Egan. Don't you forget it. If he gets uppity, that's his business."

Egan bristled at the rebuke but did not show it. "I'll take a couple of the boys with me over to Lionel's place and bring those mustangs in."

Jacob fitted a cotton square to the end of the rod, dipped it into the solvent and began running it up and down the bore of the Winchester. "You do that. We need to get 'em shod and broke to a saddle for the drive. I also want you to send a rider out to the line shack on Castle Mountain to tell Harley we are going to be moving those cows down from summer pasture in a couple of weeks for the drive."

"I'll send Weatherby. Anything else?"

Jacob turned his attention back to the rifle. "Have you seen Felicity today?"

Egan stiffened. "Saw her outside a few minutes ago." He wondered why John Jacob had asked that.

"Oh?" He ran a dry cloth through the bore, then slipped a piece of white paper in the open breech and turned it toward a window so the daylight could reflect up the barrel. The window opened to the side of the house. Beyond it Egan caught a glimpse of Peter Blake toting a long ladder toward the tree, and Rachel standing there, looking up into the branches. Jacob squinted into the barrel and said, "I've been looking for her. If you should see her again, tell her so, hm?"

"Yes, Mr. Jacob. If I happen to see her," he said, suddenly uneasy.

John Jacob levered the bolt shut and thumbed nine bullets into the magazine. "There, that's all done. All ready to go."

"Go?"

"Never know when you're going to have a need to

23

use it." Jacob gave Driscoll a quick smile, then leaned the rifle against the wall near the door and accompanied the foreman into the parlor. "You see to those jobs, now."

"Right away." They stepped out onto the porch, and Egan left the owner of the Lazy J standing in front of the stone house as he started toward the bunkhouse. Then he remembered Blake. Egan Driscoll stopped and strode toward the back of the ranch house.

"Blake! I told you to muck out that barn!"

The young man peered down at him from the upper rungs of the ladder. "Yes, sir. But Miss Jacob, she come and asked me to help her put a baby bird back into its nest."

Driscoll glared at Rachel, then at Blake, whose head and arms were hidden in the branches. "I swear the two of you are a pair. Blake, you're about as much help around this ranch as a woman. What kind of man are you, going along with this girl's foolishness? Now get your worthless hide down off that ladder and back to work. Or do I need to hold your hand and show you how to use a shovel and wheelbarrow."

"Mr. Driscoll! That's uncalled for," Rachel snapped, eyes bulging angrily. "I asked Peter to help me and he was kind enough to oblige. He's certainly more of a gentleman than you'll ever be."

Egan swung back, then stopped, fighting down a rage that made him want to slap some respect into the girl. "You just watch that mouth of yours, you brassy frog!"

Peter scrambled down the ladder. "Mr. Driscoll, that ain't no way to talk to a lady," he said in her defense.

Driscoll sprang around and his fist shot out. He was aching to hit somebody, and Peter Blake was going to be the one. Blake's head snapped back and he hit the ground. The foreman took a step toward the young man, but Rachel threw herself between them.

"Stop it! Stop it right now!"

"Out of my way, you—"

"Egan!" Felicity Jacob was suddenly standing there, a basket of fresh-cut flowers over one arm and a hard glare in her stern eyes. "That's enough of this. I'm sure my husband did not pass along orders for you to beat up the hired hands."

Egan stared at her, then at the young man sprawled on the ground. Rachel went to Blake and helped him sit up. Blake was stunned, holding his jaw in both hands.

"Let me take a look," she said, gently removing one of his hands and probing the jawbone with a finger.

"I expect the men under my charge to follow orders," Egan told Felicity. "This is the second time today that kid hasn't finished a job that was given to him."

"I requested his help," Rachel shot back. "You have no right treating anyone like this."

"What do you know about anything? You sit around all day feeding your blasted birds, reading your books or going out for your evening rides. Now you've even got my hands coddling those worthless creatures. Blake wasn't much of a man to begin with, and you've just made him worse. He's soft, like a woman. I don't need his kind around. Gather your stuff and pull out, Blake. I'll find a real man to take your place!"

"Egan, that is quite enough," Felicity said firmly, scowling.

Rachel was stunned by Driscoll's bitterness. Blake was still too much in shock to fully comprehend what was happening around him.

The commotion had drawn some of the hands over

to see what was going on. Casey Owen stepped past them, looked down at Blake, then at Driscoll. He shook his head and gave Blake a hand up. He shot a narrow look at Driscoll. His contempt was plain. With a shake of his head he looked away and helped Blake across the yard to the bunkhouse.

"What are you all looking at?" Driscoll barked. "If you haven't got nothing better to do, I'm sure I can round something up for you to do."

The men knew when to keep quiet and when to snap to. They began to drift off, but Driscoll called one of them over. "Weatherby, come here."

"Mr. Driscoll?"

"I want you to ride over to Castle Mountain. Tell Harley we are going to be driving those cows down next week. Need to start branding the calves and the mavericks. Mr. Jacob wants them ready to drive to the railhead."

"Yes, sir," Weatherby said. "I'll leave right away."

"Was that necessary?" Felicity asked when the hands had gone.

"Necessary? I don't know, but it had a right nice feel to it." Driscoll flexed the fingers of his right hand and grinned.

"You're a savage," Rachel said, turning in disgust. She stopped and looked back at her mother, then at Egan, and her eyes hardened; then she wheeled away and marched toward the house and disappeared inside.

"Think she knows?"

Felicity shook her head. "I pray to God not." Her view narrowed. "I don't know why I put up with you, Egan."

"Because you love me, and because I'm the only man here who can satisfy you. That's why."

Felicity turned her head from him.

Driscoll laughed and took her arm, but she twisted free of his hard grasp and followed her daughter into the house.

Chapter Three

Harrison Ridere wasn't ready to die—not yet, at least. It wasn't as if he could stop the buzzards from picking his bones clean if they came for him now. He just knew that if it happened today, those pearly gates folks sang about in hymns would surly be shut tight against him, and old Saint Pete would make certain there was a stout chain and padlock keeping them that way. Lying there under that burning sun, Ridere suddenly knew he could not afford to die just yet.

He'd never had much use for religion, and he marveled at how fast a man's notions change when he's looking eye to eye with the Grim Reaper.

He was drifting in and out of consciousness, struggling to keep awake. He tried focusing on his horse, which was champing the dry grass a few hundred feet away. If only he could reach it . . .

The effort made his head spin like a toy top and he

had to shut his eyes to make it stop. Then there was a sound: the crunch of a footstep on the gravely ground. He listened closer. Was it his imagination? No. He was sure of it now. Somehow, Walter Hodgeback must have trailed him here! Ridere parted his eyelids, but the glare of the sun shut them on him. Someone came around the boulder and stopped.

Ridere grabbed for his gun.

The clatter of a Winchester's lever being cycled stopped his hand. "Keep yo' hand away from dat gun, mister." It was a deep voice, easy but firm, and Ridere knew at once that it did not belong to Walter Hodgeback.

He shaded his eyes and opened them again. A man stood there, his form wavering before his eyes as if behind a curtain of shimmering heat. "Who are you?" Ridere managed.

"Heard yo' gunshot and come a'looking. Then I see this horse acting nervous, so I says 'Der am a man about here, and he am in trouble.'"

"Trouble. You got that right. Rattlesnake got me good. I plugged the sonuvabitch, but it was too late."

"Where?"

"My leg." Ridere moved it slightly, wincing at the pain.

"Lemme take a look." The man came over and laid the rifle aside.

Ridere felt the cool touch of a knife blade against his skin as the man sliced open the leg of his trousers.

"Hm. "Yo' am right. He got yo' good. It am already beginning to swell up like a watermelon. Yo' hold still. This am gonna hurt a mite."

"I'm already hurting—" Ridere stiffened suddenly and bit down on his lip, tasting blood.

"Told yo' so."

The man sucked the poison from the wound, then left him there while he caught Ridere's horse. "I'm gonna put yo' atop your horse and take yo' into town."

"No. No, I can't go back to town."

"Why?" He heard the suspicion in the man's voice.

Ridere might have fetched up a clever story to tell him if he'd been of a clear mind to do so, but right then all he could do was tell it straight and hope the man would understand. "I'm being hunted by the law."

"What did yo' do? Yo' didn't kill no one, did yo'?"

"No, nothing like that."

"Rob a store?"

"No. I"—he hesitated, wondering how to say it—"I cuckolded the sheriff."

The man threw back his head and roared with laughter. "Yo' bedded Sheriff Hodgeback's wife?"

"Yeah, I guess you might say that."

"Well, yo' ain't the first one, and yo' ain't gonna be the last, from what I hear of that filly." The man helped Ridere to his feet and onto the saddle. "I'll take yo' to my place for a couple days until yo' am feeling a little better. Dat leg of yo' am gonna swell something fierce. Just hope I don't have to cut it off a week from now."

"Cut it off!"

"It can happen."

Ridere clutched the horn. It was a struggle to keep himself in place. "What is your name? You never said." His vision had not cleared much, but he could tell the man was a burly fellow and his skin was blacker than a velvet pall at midnight.

"Lionel is my name. And yo'?"

"Harrison Ridere. Harry, for short."

"All right, Mr. Harry. Yo' come along with me now." Lionel grabbed up the reins to his horse and started off into the rugged hills that broke up the land, rolling away to the mountains beyond.

Riding a little ahead of the others, John Russell Keane spied the sheriff first. He threw up his hand and brought the men to a halt. Old habits die hard. Keane had spent more than half his life as an army officer, working his way to the rank of major before an "incident" had forced his retirement. It was either that or face a court-martial. Since Keane had begun riding with O'Brian, Louvel, Nantaje and Ridere, he just naturally took over the leadership role. No one appeared to mind very much. A tenuous friendship held these men together, and sometimes even that wasn't nearly up to the task. None of them had any ties to any one place, and since traveling was what they did best, traveling together made life just that much more interesting.

Through a fortunate skirmish down in Mexico with the criminal family headed by Gaspar Ortega some months back, money was no longer a problem for them. They each carried a bag of silver, and so far those bags were still mostly full. That couldn't last forever. Someday they'd have to find work. Each man knew that, and each in his own way was pondering the inevitable. Talking it over among themselves, California seemed to be a pleasant place to end up, and if this group of outcasts could be said to have a common goal at all, it was to someday reach the western edge of this wide country and put down roots.

But the road to California did not run swift or true, and somehow it had managed to wind its way here, into southern Colorado.

"Looks like the sheriff is coming back," Keane said.

"Is Harry with him?" Dougal O'Brian asked, lifting himself in the stirrups for a better look.

"No."

Royden Louvel said in a soft southern drawl, "That boy has more lives than a cat."

"Ridere could have lost himself almost anywhere in this land. It is cut by canyons and ravines like the wrinkles on an old man's face." Nantaje, the ex-scout for General Crook, studied the land that stretched away all around them. Utah lay not far to the west; Arizona and New Mexico territories just to the south. It was a dry, desolate place, mainly good for ranching so long as you could afford a hundred acres of it just to support one cow. The ranches in this area were immense.

"Here he comes," O'Brian said quietly.

"Let me do the talking," Louvel said.

Walter Hodgeback drew rein and gave each of them a quick once-over, his scowl lingering a mite longer on Nantaje. "What sort of Injun are you? You sure ain't Ute, and you don't look Comanch either."

"Apache," Nantaje said.

"Hm. Kinda far north, ain't you?"

"We are traveling together, suh," Louvel said.

Hodgeback's view shifted and found Louvel's missing right arm. "Traveling where?"

"California."

Hodgeback raked in his lower lip with his teeth and began worrying it. "You boys are sorta headed the wrong way for California, ain't you? This road goes north and east."

"We are touring the countryside, suh."

"Oh, is that it?" Hodgeback didn't sound convinced. "Where did you lose that arm, mister?"

"Gaines's Mills."

"Figured it must have been the war. And to hear your

manner of speaking, I don't have to ask which side you fought for."

Hodgeback was a blunt man, rough in manner and appearance. He was of medium height, thick about the waist and fleshy in the face. His skin was dark from the sun, his eyes a pale shade of green. He had shaved recently, and had nicked his chin and missed some whiskers down his neck. He peeled back his vest and showed them the badge pinned on his shirt beneath it. "I'm looking for a man. Young, maybe mid-twenties. Kinda light hair. He was wearing an old pair of army trousers, light shirt and a black vest. He lit outa town about half an hour ago. None of you boys happened to see him, did you?"

"Light hair, you say? Black vest?"

"That's right."

Louvel looked at his partners. "Any of you see this fellow the sheriff is hunting?"

"I seen a fellow who looked like that back in Mariposa Springs," O'Brian said, scratching his cheek beneath his shaggy graying beard. "Was with a woman, as I recollect, a good-looking woman."

"That's the man!" Hodgeback's eyes narrowed in anticipation. "You didn't see him come along the road here, did you?"

"Can't say as I have."

"How 'bout you?" Hodgeback demanded of Keane.

"You're the first person we've seen since riding out of town, Sheriff," he replied honestly.

"Ah'm afraid we can't help you, Sheriff."

Hodgeback glared at Louvel and a low growl seemed to rumble deep down in his throat. "I'll find the sonuvabitch, and when I do, I'll . . . I'll . . ." He suddenly went silent and composed himself. "If any of you

33

boys happen to find him and bring him to me, I'll see to it you get something for your trouble."

"Ah will keep that in mind, Sheriff. Might Ah ask the man's name?"

"Don't know his name—yet." Hodgeback's eyes narrowed toward the town, laying some few miles in the distance. "But I intend to find out directly." The ruthless determination in his voice sent a cool shiver up Keane's spine. Keane understood men, and he realized just then that this man was capable of anything. And standing behind a sheriff's badge, he could probably get away with anything.

Louvel said, "What is the man wanted for, Sheriff?"

"The sonuvabitch went and—" Again Hodgeback caught himself and reined in his rage some. "He's wanted for disturbing the peace." Hodgeback clucked his horse into motion and started toward the distant town.

"There goes one dangerous man," Keane noted.

O'Brian gave a short laugh. "Disturbing the peace. Did you hear?"

"Ah wonder how he intended that?"

They looked at Louvel.

"Ah mean the 'peace' Ridere disturbed. Do you suppose it was spelled p-e-a-c-e, or p-i-e-c-e?"

The men laughed, all except Nantaje. Keane explained it to him. "I reckon we'll have to search for Harry," Keane went on, surveying the land around them. "He could be anywhere."

"Harry is in hiding, that's for sure," O'Brian said. "And it's a sure thing he won't be sticking his nose out anytime soon, so long as that fellow is hounding his trail."

"Think you can track him, Nantaje?" Keane asked.

The Apache scout nodded. "Already have been, John

Russell." He pointed at the hard-packed road. "His tracks are there." Nantaje slipped off his horse and hunkered over some impressions, tracing one of them with a finger. "The shoe on the left rear is set slightly off."

"You can see that?" Since they all had started riding together, O'Brian never ceased to be surprised by the Apache. Nantaje could pick out subtle differences in even the most ordinary of things; an odor, the angle of a broken twig, the moisture left in a patch of trampled grass . . . or a horseshoe not set correctly by a farrier.

Nantaje swung back on his horse and started off ahead of them, moving slowly, his dark eyes reading the signs. Every now and then he would leave the road and ride in lazy circles, then return and push on.

Keane understood that tracking was a slow business, but in his years as an army officer during the Apache wars, he had come to respect an Apache scout's abilities. He had no doubt that Ridere had left the road at some point, or that Nantaje would discover exactly where eventually.

Lionel's cabin had only one room, built of logs and tucked down inside a pretty little canyon where a clear stream flowed through stands of ancient cottonwood trees. Not far below the front door a small barn sat off to one side of the cabin, along with several acres of fencing enclosing four or five corrals. Ridere was barely awake when they arrived, but he did note the horses. There might have been twenty of them, separated out among three of the paddocks.

Lionel helped him off the horse. The cabin was sparsely furnished; two chairs, a table, a small one-burner cook stove and three plank shelves holding an assortment of canned goods and boxes. There was a single window in the place, and along one wall was a sagging rope bed on four posts driven into the dirt floor. Lionel laid him onto the thin mattress and brought over a ladle of cool water and gave him some to drink. Then he began to clean the wound that had already turned the color of raw meat.

"Swelling up mighty ugly, ain't it?" Ridere said.

"Um-um, dat serpent got yo' real good," Lionel said.

"He was big."

"This country grows 'em dat way, Mr. Harry. Might just have to lance it before the skin busts wide open."

Ridere's head had stopped spinning. He was tired, and sleep began to pull heavy at his eyelids. "I sure am grateful you found me, Lionel," he said, smacking his dry lips a couple of times and running his tongue over them.

Lionel helped him with another drink of water. "We'll see how dat leg looks in another hour or two before I decide what to do with it."

"You live out here all by yourself?"

"Yep. Just me and my horses. Sometimes de hands from de ranch come by to bring me more, and sometimes they don't. Me, I like it this way. Don't like too many folks crowding in." He laughed. "And for de most part, they don't like crowding too close to me neither, no sir."

"Why is that?" Ridere asked.

"Why? Can't yo' see? I is colored!" Lionel shook his head, as if his explanation should have been crystal clear from the start.

"Where is this place?"

"We am on Lazy J land. Mr. John Jacob, he owns all this land as far as de eye can see. He got a place about five, six miles from here." Lionel gave a short laugh. "Mr. Jacob, he make sure I was far away from where he spreads his blanket. But he treats me all right. I've known worse."

"All those horses in the corrals yours?"

"They belong to Mr. Jacob. Yo' see, I break them horses he brings me, and I do it better than any man around these parts. So he's got to treat me good."

Ridere was drifting off, but he heard Lionel say, "Need to check up on my horses. I'll put your animal away an' give him some oats. Looks like yo' rode him hard. Then I'll rustle us up some grub, Mr. Harry."

Sunlight was cutting low through the window when Ridere opened his eyes. He'd slept most of the day away, and now the late sun cast a rectangle of light against the back wall, picking out the rough surface of the logs in fine detail. Outside the cabin he heard the sound of water being poured into something, then splashing. Presently he became aware of a low, deep tone, as of a man singing softly to himself. It was Lionel's voice. He relaxed then and looked about for his gun. It and his holster were hanging from a peg near the door.

The door opened and Lionel stepped in, rubbing his face and hair in a towel. He was naked from his narrow waist up to his broad shoulders and drops of water glistened on his black skin. Lionel was of an indeterminable age, but Ridere made him out to be in his mid-thirties, maybe a bit more.

"Ho, yo' am awake, Mr. Harry," he said, as if pleasantly surprised by that. "Lemme take a look at dat leg." He tossed the towel over the back of a chair and bent over him. Ridere didn't want to look and stared at the open rafters of the ceiling instead. "Hmm. Might have to lance it yet," Lionel said, gently probing the puffy skin around the bite wound with a finger.

"You ever treat a snake bite before, Lionel?"

"Oh, sure. I done it a time or two."

"You ever know a man to . . . die from one?"

Lionel gave a laugh and a wide grin spread his cheeks. "Yo' am not gonna die, Mr. Harry. Men don't generally die from a rattler's bite. Oh, it do happen, but not often. Nope, they just get mighty sick and wish they would die. But every man I heard of who have been bitten will say the same thing. They say they keep some feel of the serpent's bite all de rest of der life.

"I did see a man lose a couple of fingers once. A little bitty ol' swamp rattler got him right in de skin between his thumb and finger. His hand, it done puffed up bigger than Injun squash. Looked all dark red at first, then started to turn black. De marster finally took him in to see a doctor, and right off that doc done cut them two fingers right off. Doc say if he'd waited another couple days, he'd have died from poisoned blood. Dat was near as I ever see a man die from a snake bite. An' it was just a little bitty snake!"

Ridere gulped and closed his eyes. He was suddenly thinking of Royden Louvel's missing arm. "Am I going to lose the leg?"

"Too early to tell, but I don't think it will come to dat. I got most de poison out. And if we lance it, maybe de skin won't up and perish like it done to dat other fellow I was telling yo' about."

Lionel stood. "I'll go see if I can't shoot us a couple rabbits or squirrels to eat, Mr. Harry." When he turned and reached for the shirt hanging off the corner of one of the shelves Ridere saw the scars that crisscrossed his back. They looked at first as if someone had taken a piece of chalk and played a wild game of ticktacktoe upon his black skin.

"What happened to you?"

Lionel looked back as he shrugged into the shirt. "Another time and another place, Mr. Harry. I don't think about it anymore."

"You were a slave?"

"I was, but I ain't no more," he said flatly. He took a rifle from the corner, levered open the breech bolt halfway, glanced at the gleam of brass, closed it and thumbed the hammer to half-cock. "I'll be back directly," he said, reaching for the door.

"Hey, Lionel."

The black man turned.

"Just want to thank you for what you're doing."

"No need. I know what it feels like to be on the run."

"You do?"

"Yo' don't think I waited for no white man to sign no papers before I got my freedom?"

"You ran away?"

He laughed. "Running away had become my stock and trade, Mr. Harry. How do yo' think I got all them scars anyway? I earned every one of them. But when I finally made it to the Indian Territory, it was worth every stripe them overseers ever give to me. Now, yo' just rest. Yo' am safe here." Lionel left, closing the door behind him.

Ridere tried to sit up, but the effort made him sick and his head began spinning again. Gently, he eased himself back onto the bed and closed his eyes.

Chapter Four

"Corey. Hep. Get your horses and come along with me," Egan Driscoll called through the open door to the bunkhouse.

Corey Lomis swung his legs off the cot and grabbed his hat. "Where we going, boss?"

Driscoll shot a burning look at Casey Owen, who was helping Peter Blake nurse a swollen jaw. "We're going to finish the job that didn't get done this morning." His words were meant for Casey, and he wasn't hiding his contempt. "And if that nigger gets uppity with me, I'll cut him down a notch or two and put him back in his place."

"Lionel ain't a man to take any guff, not from you, Driscoll, or anyone else," Casey said.

"We'll see about that."

"Getting kinda late, ain't it?" Hep Johnson said, squinting out the window at the long shadows that lay across the yard, slowly beginning to swallow the huge barn.

"Mr. Jacob wants those horses here today. We have to get saddles on their backs and see that they are trail ready this week."

"What if Lionel is still away?" Hep asked.

"Then we'll just take them without his *permission*. No uppity nigger is gonna tell me what I can or can't do—on Lazy J land, or anywhere else. Now let's get moving. I don't want to spend all night moving those animals. I got plans for later on."

"Plans? What sort of plans do you have away out here?" Corey wondered.

"That ain't none of your business, now is it, Lomis?" Driscoll swung away from the open door and strode off toward the barn.

Corey and Hep looked at each other and Hep gave him a shrug. "That man sure grates, don't he?"

"He's the boss," Lomis said flatly in Driscoll's defense.

"Yeah. He's the boss. But I sure don't know how he got that job." Hep glanced at Casey. "How come Mr. Jacob didn't make you foreman, Casey? You deserved it more than that swaggering popinjay."

Casey looked over, a tight smile fixed on his weathered face. "Maybe it's because I didn't say the right words to the right people. And maybe those people don't put in a good word on my account because of that."

"What is that supposed to mean, Casey?" Lomis shot back.

"That means exactly what Driscoll told you. It's none of your business."

* * *

41

Peter Blake stood before John Jacob's big oak desk and shook his head. "I appreciate the offer, Mr. Jacob, but I can't stay and work for that man any longer. Driscoll treats the men like dirt, then he wonders why they don't work for him. I know it ain't none of my business, but if this was my ranch, I'd get me a new foreman."

Jacob frowned. "I appreciate your feelings, Peter. I wish you'd stay on, but I understand what you're saying." He cleared his throat and lowered his voice, glancing out the open office door. Felicity was in the parlor and there was a flourish of her skirts as she swept past the doorway and disappeared down the hall. He glanced back. "Things are about to change. They have to. I've had complaints from several of the men. If you'd just stick it out until after the drive . . ."

"Driscoll already fired me."

"Dammit, it's my ranch, not his. I'm hiring you back."

Blake frowned and shook his head. "I can't stay. Not so long as he's still around. Sorry, Mr. Jacob."

Jacob snorted out a sharp breath. "I understand. Give it a month or two, then if you change your mind, come on back. We might have made some changes around here by then."

Blake nodded, fingering the brim of his hat as he stood there. "I'll give it some thought."

"You do that." Jacob rose from the desk chair and retrieved a steel box from the safe and counted out the pay Blake had coming to him. Afterward, he accompanied him outside, where his horse was waiting with a bedroll and everything Blake owned tied behind the cantle. The scarred butt of a Winchester peeked out from its saddle scabbard, half hidden beneath a small duffel bag hanging from the horn.

"Take care." Jacob offered a hand. Blake took it, then stepped up into the saddle.

"Thank you, Mr. Jacob."

John Jacob glanced back into the house through the open door. Felicity was standing in the parlor, watching both of them. "Er, good luck, Peter." Jacob went back into the house and closed the door.

Blake started down the road toward the tall portal at the edge of the yard. Before he had passed under the wide cross timber with the Lazy J name carved into it, Rachel Jacob rode from around the back of the barn and reined a lineback buckskin mare to a halt beside him.

"Rachel?" Blake was surprised but pleased that she would come and see him off.

"It's not fair what Driscoll did to you, Pete," she said all at once, as if what had happened to him was her all-consuming thought. "It wasn't your fault. I asked for your help. That man has no right doing what he does around here!" she said hotly.

"I know. But I learned a long time ago that life wasn't fair, Miss Rachel." He tried to grin and winced at the pain in his face.

"Your eye is all swollen. Does it hurts real bad?"

"Eye, jaw—they both hurt." He managed to laugh. "But the pain will pass."

She stretched out a hand and gently touched the swollen skin. "I'm sorry. It's all my fault." Her voice was suddenly soft and filled with deep regret. He didn't know what to make of Rachel's sudden show of feeling toward him except that just then he wanted to reach out and pull her close to him. But all he could manage was to touch her fingers. They lingered a moment upon his face before being withdrawn.

"Won't you change your mind?"

Blake shook his head. "So long as that man is here, I can't stay."

Rachel blinked and brushed at a glint of moisture before glancing away. When she looked back the tears were gone, replaced with a look that Blake could not read. "I understand," she said flatly. There was just a hint of resignation in her voice—or was it sadness? He couldn't be sure.

He tried to grin again. "You take care of all your critters, Miss Rachel."

"I will. I'll miss your bringing me grain from the barn like you used to."

A lump rose in his throat and he knew if he lingered much longer there would be moisture in his eyes too. "I'll miss that too. Good-bye." He wanted to say more but couldn't and touched his spurs to his horse's flanks. As he left Rachel there watching him ride away, he felt his melancholy turn to anger, and that anger burned red hot against the man who had caused his heart to be ripped from his chest and left laying on the road.

Blake cast a final glance over his shoulder. Rachel's horse was now standing at the hitching rail in front of the stone ranch house, and she was gone. Then the road made a dip and the Lazy J disappeared from view. Peter Blake felt suddenly alone, and he was mad.

Harrison Ridere drifted in and out of sleep while Lionel was away hunting for dinner. He thought about Carla Hodgeback and the other women who had passed so freely through his life, and in a dreamy way he heard Royden Louvel's voice inside his head, warning him that his wayward lifestyle would bring him to a bad end someday. When he heard the sounds of horses riding up outside he came suddenly alert. Ridere feared that Sheriff Walter Hodgeback had finally tracked him down. He glanced at his gun on the peg across the room.

"Lionel? Lionel, are you inside there?" a man barked impatiently.

Ridere bolted up off the pillow. The rapid movement made his head whirl, and he had to reach out for the wall to steady himself.

"Looks like he still ain't back, Mr. Driscoll," another voice said.

A third man spoke up. "Just like Casey said. He's gone off somewhere."

"It don't matter if he's here or not, we are going to take those horses back with us, and if Lionel says anything, he'll be sorry."

"Lionel takes his job seriously, Mr. Driscoll." This was the third voice. "He's liable to be a handful if he takes it in his head to get his nose outa whack."

Driscoll said, "Let the son of a bitch raise a stink. I'll kick his black ass off this range like I done Blake."

Ridere tried to stand. The room lurched beneath his feet. He sat back on the bed and scooted along to its foot, where he had a narrow view through a slit in the faded blue curtains. Three men on horseback sat there in the gathering dusk. A wave of relief washed over him. Walter Hodgeback was not one of them.

"Lionel!" the first man, the one called Driscoll, an older gent with a craggy, sunburned face and a hard look in his deep-set eyes, called again. He turned to the two with him, one a young fellow in a gray vest and gray hat, the other older and bigger. They all had the lean, tough look of wranglers. "Get those mustangs out of the corrals and ready to move. I'll check out the cabin."

"Right, boss," the older of the two said, and they rode toward the barn.

Driscoll stepped down off his horse. Tall and scowling like a Comanche, he started for the house.

Just then Lionel's deep voice boomed from somewhere nearby. "I thought that was you."

Driscoll swung around. Ridere couldn't see the black man, but he heard him. "What am yo' doing here, Mr. Egan? Yo' and Johnson and Lomis?"

"Came to take the mustangs. Mr. Jacob has been waiting for them. You are more than a week late on bringing 'em in, Lionel."

From where he was sitting on the bed, watching out the window, Ridere saw Lionel step into view with a long-legged jackrabbit dangling by the ears in one hand and his rifle in the other, resting upon his shoulder.

"They ain't ready to go yet, Mr. Egan. Ain't got 'em full broke yet."

"I'm taking them anyway."

"Nobody touches my horses till I say they am ready to go. Tell de boys I'll bring them mustangs in when they am ready."

"They aren't your horses, Lionel. Don't know why you can't get that through your thick black head. And they are going tonight. Mr. Jacob's orders." Driscoll started for the corrals.

Lionel dropped the rabbit and grabbed him by the shirtsleeve.

Driscoll rounded without warning. His fist knocked Lionel to the ground. The rifle landed a few feet away and Lionel sat there, shaking his head. Then, like a bull bolting from a pen, he was up and driving hard with his shoulder. He rammed the taller man, buckling him in the middle. The two tumbled across the ground, Lionel on top, then Driscoll. There was blood on both men's faces when they finally separated and scrambled to their feet and began to circle.

Ridere heard the men down by the corral coming up to watch the fight.

The two combatants circled some more. . . .

Then all at once a gunshot rang out nearby. There was a muzzle flash from the trees down by the stream and Driscoll lurched at Lionel and slammed hard to the ground.

Stunned, Lionel stood there a second, then dove for his rifle, levering a shell into the chamber as he came about, crouched low, swinging toward the dark line of trees down by the water. At that moment the two wranglers came rushing around the corner of the cabin. They drew up, stared at Driscoll laying there, then at Lionel and his rifle in his fists.

"What the hell did you do to him, Lionel?" the older fellow exclaimed.

Lionel swung toward them, eyes wide with fear, forgetting that he was still holding the gun.

"Duck, Hep!" the younger one shouted, drawing the revolver he carried in a battered holster on his belt.

Hep hit the ground, clawing his own gun from its holster.

Lionel just stood there, the shock and fear on his face turning to confusion. His eyes darted between the wranglers and the dark line of cottonwood trees below the cabin.

Ridere had caught his breath. He watched it all from the cabin window, hardly believing what he was seeing.

"Drop the rifle, Lionel," the young one cried, fear and panic rising dangerously in his voice as he leveled his gun. "Drop it now, or I swear I'll do to you like you done Mr. Driscoll!"

"What yo' say, Lomis?" Lionel croaked. He was suddenly aware of how the cards had shifted on him.

"You heard him," Hep said, holding steady on Lionel with a solid two-handed grip. Both men were spooked. Lionel too. Ridere felt like he was sitting on one of Dougal O'Brian's dynamite crates back down in Mexico again.

Lionel lowered the Winchester. "I didn't shoot him!"

"Drop it! All the way!" Lomis ordered.

Lionel reach back and leaned the rifle against the cabin wall. He looked at the guns pointed his way and said, "I didn't do it."

Hep said, "We heard you two scrapping. We heard the shot. And there you are holding a rifle. How dumb do you take us for, Lionel? Now, step away from the rifle, out here in the open where we can watch you better."

"I didn't do it!" Lionel insisted and moved a few paces to his right.

The men on the ground stood, keeping him covered.

Lomis said, "Check the rifle, Hep."

Hep picked it up and smelled the muzzle. "It's been fired."

"I just shot me a rabbit to eat," Lionel told him.

"Looks to me like you shot more than that," Lomis said, kneeling over Driscoll's body. "He's dead, Hep."

"What are we gonna do about it?" Hep wondered aloud.

"Reckon we got to take Lionel back with us and let Mr. Jacob figure that out," Lomis said.

"I ain't going with yo'! I didn't shoot him. While we am wasting time here, Mr. Egan's killer am getting away!"

Lomis frowned. "I don't know what to think. What do you think, Hep?"

"I reckon if I just killed a man, I'd be singing the same tune, trying to put us on a wild goose chase so as I could light a shuck for the mountains and hide out."

"But I didn't do it!"

Lomis said, "We're gonna take you back to the ranch. You can tell Mr. Jacob you didn't do it."

"Yo' ain't gonna put a rope on me!"

"Don't make me have to use this gun, Lionel," Hep said, trying to reason with the man.

Ridere had seen enough. Lionel was innocent and it was time he told them exactly what had happened. But when he stood, his head went spinning like a top again. He felt suddenly sick, and his vision blurred. He grabbed for the back of one of the chairs, but his eyes were playing tricks on him. The chair wasn't where they said it should be. He tried to catch himself as he fell and struck his head upon its seat . . . and then everything went black.

Chapter Five

It was black as the belly of a cave inside the cabin when he finally came to. Groggily, Ridere sat up and hit his head against the table. He sat perfectly still and listened, and looked around. The window was a slightly less black rectangle to his right, and when he got his eyes to focus he saw the star-filled night sky beyond it. No sounds of danger came from out there, just the far-off howl of a coyote and the whisper of a breeze as a chill night wind stirred the frayed ends of the curtains.

"How did I get here?" he wondered aloud as his eyes adjusted to the dim light through the window. He rubbed his head and fingered the goose egg that hadn't been there before. Then he remembered; the fight, the shooting, his fall, which had made whatever followed a complete blank in his brain. He could only suppose that Lionel had been taken back to the ranch. And unless he had been able to convince the owner he was innocent, Lionel was probably sitting in Walter Hodgeback's jail right now.

Grabbing the table, he pulled himself up and stood there waiting for the room to stop spinning. The poison was still in his blood, and his leg felt as if it was about to burst. Lionel had said his leg might need lancing, and if it wasn't lanced, he might lose it. A thought suddenly occurred to Ridere: What if he had to do the job himself? How could he? He didn't know nor did he know how he would take proper care of the wound in his state.

His head cleared some and he remembered his gun. He felt the need to have it nearby and worked his way to the holster on the peg. Then he hobbled to the bed and eased himself to the pillow. Lionel was in trouble, big trouble, and Ridere wanted to help. But how could he, laid up like this, barely able to make his way across the room, let alone to the ranch, which might be in any direction? One thing was certain—he couldn't go to Sheriff Hodgeback with his story. No, there had to be another way. But right then all he could think about was the burning ache in his leg and the throbbing goose egg on his head.

"Morning. Wait till morning," he told himself, licking parched lips and wondering if Lionel had left any water in the cabin. There was a stream down below, but in his condition it might as well have been in California!

California, he thought with a wave of despair. Was he ever going to reach that far western land? The way he felt now, he had his doubts.

Then there was the sound of hooves outside the window. Ridere stiffened, listening. Horses were approaching. He felt on the bed for the holster, thumbed off the safety thong and slipped the Colt free of the leather. Maybe it was only some of Lionel's mustangs, busted loose of the corrals and wandering about the place.

His ears strained at the faint sounds coming from the window. There was a creak of saddle leather, followed by the faint thud of a foot touching the ground. It wasn't the mustangs. Horsemen!

Ridere's heart thumped faster as footsteps approached the cabin. His fist tightened around the revolver. It had to be the sheriff. Maybe Lionel had told the sheriff he was here. Hodgeback had finally found him. Ridere was sure of it!

With daylight fading from the sky, Nantaje finally struck upon Ridere's trail. He had left the road at a place where a slab of sandstone lay exposed by the wind. Fortunate for him, because the sheriff had completely overlooked the faint signs. But the Apache scout saw them, and once past the rock the trail was a simple matter to follow. The men dismounted among the sandstone boulders, found the place Ridere had waited and came upon the dead snake, partly shredded by the ravens that had feasted on it.

"A second man now," Nantaje noted, studying a confusion of tracks. "They go this way. One is helping the other."

"Who is being helped?" Keane asked.

"It is Harry, John Russell."

"That serpent must have got him," O'Brian surmised, scowling behind the fierce gray beard.

Nantaje nodded. "He is putting all his weight on his right foot."

"What about the second man?" Royden Louvel asked, his dark eyes surveying the rugged land.

"He a big man. Comes down heavy on his heels

when he walks and rolls to the outside of his feet with each step. Like a man who spends much time on horseback. Look, they mount up here and ride away to the north."

"Then that's the way we go," Keane said swinging back onto his horse.

Nantaje took the lead again, following Harrison Ridere's trail into the coming night.

It was well after dark when they spied the dark shape of a cabin buried down among the deeper night shadows in a valley below.

Keane said, "You two stay here. Nantaje and I will see if anyone is down there."

"There are horses in the corrals, but I don't see any lights burning," O'Brian said.

"They could be asleep. You go riding down there unannounced, you're liable to be greeted with a bullet," Louvel warned.

"I'll try to avoid that, Mr. Louvel," Keane said and softly clucked his horse forward. They followed a well-worn trail into the valley and in the yard quietly reined to a stop. Nantaje slipped to the ground and crept to the door, putting an ear against it. After a moment he nodded and backed away.

"Hello, inside the cabin," Keane called.

No one. Keane tried again. "Anyone in there? You awake? We need to talk to you."

"Keane? Major Keane, is that you?"

"Harry?"

"It's me!"

"You alone?"

"I am. Am I glad to hear your voice!"

Keane nodded. Nantaje tried the door. It swung open, and the Apache went inside. Keane dismounted

53

and cast a glance around the place, making certain no one else was lurking about before following Nantaje inside. He struck a match. Ridere was sitting on a bed, his back against the wall, his gun wrapped tightly in his fingers. Keane found a lamp on a shelf and lit the wick.

"You all right?"

"Not really, but I'll live. The granddaddy of all rattlers took a piece of me."

"We saw it. Who brought you here? Where is he?"

"A man named Lionel found me. Doctored me the best he could. Then some men came by. There was a fight, and one of them got shot. The others took Lionel away with them. I went to help him, but I didn't make it. Knocked myself silly on the edge of that chair instead. Only come to a few minutes ago." He rubbed the knot on his head. "How did you find me?"

"Nantaje tracked you."

"Should have guessed." Ridere glanced at the Apache. "Thanks."

Nantaje examined Ridere's swollen leg while Keane stepped outside and signaled the others to come on in. Ridere told them what had happened, from the time Sheriff Hodgeback had caught him in the arms of his wife up until the moment he'd lost consciousness.

"When I heard you ride up, I thought it was Hodgeback. I can't tell you what a relief it was to hear your voice."

Royden Louvel gave a short laugh and said, "Ah told you to watch yourself. Fooling around with other men's women is a sure ticket for a fast train on a short track to the grave."

"I know, I know. Been thinking a lot about what you said since this all started."

O'Brian laughed. "Don't pay him no mind, Harry.

I've been run outa more towns than I can count because of one woman or another. You just gotta be faster on your feet than her husband, is all."

"I don't know, Dougal. I'm getting mighty weary of keeping one step ahead of a gelding knife or six-gun. A furious father or a gunning husband. Maybe Captain Louvel is right."

"Aye, lad, I've thought of giving it up myself a time or two. I'd go to the priest, get absolution and do my penance, but then the next week I'd be chasing them skirts and sinning all over again. And you will be too. It's in your blood!"

Ridere frowned.

Nantaje was studying the swollen leg. "This not look good, Harry."

"That's what Lionel kept saying. Said he might have to lance it or I could lose the leg." Ridere glanced at the pinned-up empty shirtsleeve dangling where Louvel's right arm used to be. "I don't want to lose it."

"If skin starts to die, you might," Nantaje said.

Ridere nodded. "Do what needs doing," he said, looking worried and ready to endure any pain to save his leg.

Keane peered over Nantaje's shoulder at it and shook his head at the sight. "When you finish up will he be able to ride?"

"He can, but he should rest a few days first."

"We should be putting some distance between us and this place."

"Ah agree with Major Keane. There is too much trouble hereabouts for my liking."

"We can't leave," Ridere said.

"Why not?" Keane asked.

"I already told you. They think Lionel killed that man. But I saw it all through the window. The shot

55

came from down by the stream. Lionel wasn't even holding a rifle when it happened! If it wasn't for him, I'd still be back there, a lot worse off than I am now. I can't just up and leave him in the mess he's in."

"Where is this man now?" Louvel asked.

"They said they were taking him back to the Lazy J's headquarters. My guess is, he's cooling his heels in Sheriff Hodgeback's jail right now."

"Lazy J?"

"That's what one of them called it."

Nantaje took out his knife and wiped the blade on his shirtsleeve.

Ridere gulped and stared. "Ain't you going to clean it better than that?"

"Knife not dirty," Nantaje said, looking at it just to be sure.

"Hold up there a minute." O'Brian headed out the door and returned a moment later with a bottle of tequila. "I hate to waste good liquor on something as frivolous as Harry's leg . . ." He peered at the bottle, then sighed. "And I'll have you know I wouldn't do this for anyone else. Here you go, Nantaje, splash a little of this on that blade—but only a little!"

The Apache frowned impatiently at all the precautions, but he'd lived among white men long enough to expect such peculiarities. He cleaned the knife, then O'Brian wetted a piece of cloth with the tequila and swabbed the swollen area of Ridere's leg.

"There. Now you can cut him," the Irishman said, taking a long pull from the bottle and smacking his lips. He offered it around and was not disappointed when no one took up his offer. O'Brian moved out of the Apache's way and tipped the bottom of the bottle toward the ceiling again.

Keane held the lantern near. Louvel watched dispassionately. Nantaje put the knife to the swollen leg and drew a long, thin, bloody line along the skin. Ridere stiffened and ground his teeth at its bite. O'Brian watched a moment, his mouth a grim line set deep within his graying beard, then he turned away and stepped outside, claiming the cabin had become mighty tight with all five of them inside.

During the night the skin peeled open wider and wider, revealing the flaming muscle beneath. Twice Nantaje had to lengthen the cut, but the release of the pressure was a relief. Ridere finally fell into a deep sleep just as the sky was brightening to the east.

The sun had been a couple of hours in the sky and J. R. Keane was outside gathering an armful of wood to heat some water when the riders appeared suddenly from a trail down past the corrals and barn. There were five of them, and they rode up to the cabin and reined in around him.

"Who are you?" a stocky man astride a tall chestnut demanded.

"The name is Keane. John Russell Keane," he said, eyeing the riders.

The door opened and Royden Louvel stepped out.

The man on the chestnut glanced at Louvel, noted the missing arm, then looked back at Keane. "You are on Lazy J land, mister. What are you doing here?"

"Who might you be?" Keane asked.

"I'm John Jacob. I own the Lazy J, and you two are trespassing."

"Ah prefer to call it a fortunate port in a storm, suh," Louvel said easily, grinning.

John Jacob obviously wasn't expecting to find anyone here. It was apparent that Lionel had not told him about Ridere. Keane figured the less he said about that, the better.

Louvel said, "If we have trespassed, we apologize." He stepped up to the horse and offered his hand. Jacob thought it over, then took it. "You see, we have a friend inside who took a bite from a rattlesnake yesterday. He's in a bad way. When we came upon the cabin it was empty, and our friend needed a place to rest. We figured the owner would be returning soon, considering all those fine horses in the corral."

The tension eased some and Jacob said, "Well, when an emergency arises a man does what needs doing. I understand how that is. We've been dealing with one ourselves. My foreman was murdered here yesterday, trying to bring those horses back to the ranch."

"Sorry to hear that," Keane said. "You know who did it?"

"We have the man. Took him into town and handed him over to the sheriff this morning." Jacob frowned and shook his head. "Never would have expected it of him. He was a good hand and the best bronc buster I ever had. But it looks like he'll swing for what he done."

Keane gave Louvel a warning glance. The Southerner knew when to keep quiet, and neither one said any more about it.

Jacob dismounted. "Let's take a look at your friend. Casey, you come with me. The rest of you men start moving those horses back to headquarters." He hooked a thumb at the tall man with him. "This here is Casey Owen. He's taken over the job of foreman now that Driscoll is dead."

Nantaje and O'Brian were inside. "Just how many of there are you?" Jacob asked, his view lingering on the Apache.

"Five," Keane told him.

Jacob studied Ridere's leg. "You got it bad, son," he said, frowning.

"Don't I know it," Ridere said.

"What are you boys doing away out here?"

"Just passing through on our way to California," Keane said.

"California, huh? That's a long piece off."

"We're in no hurry."

"Good thing. Looks like you five will be stuck in these parts for a while. I've seen snakebit men take weeks to get back on their feet. That bite looks nasty enough to keep you bed bound for a good long while." Jacob looked around the place, as if thinking it over. "Well, I've no use for this place for the rest of the season, and it doesn't look like Lionel will be having much use for it any time soon either—if ever. You boys can stay until your friend is fit enough to travel."

Keane and Louvel went back outside with them. "Appreciate your hospitality," Keane said.

"You're welcome." He turned to Louvel. "What part of the South are you from?"

"Louisiana, suh. My family had lived in New Orleans over a hundred years . . . until the damned Yankees came and we lost everything."

Jacob nodded. "I know what you mean. We lost most of our holdings after the war too. My family raised horses and cotton. I managed to salvage some of the property, sell it off and start over again out here."

Casey was considering something. He said, "You know, Mr. Jacob, now that Blake is gone, and Driscoll is dead, we are short a couple of hands. I wonder if these two would be interested in a job while they wait for their friend to recover?"

"Good idea." Jacob gave Keane and Louvel a questioning glance. "You two ever work cows?"

Louvel only laughed. "I seem to be short a hand myself. I don't think I can be of much help to you. But perhaps my Yankee friend here?"

They weren't short on money—not yet at least—but Keane figured a job on the Lazy J might put him in a position to learn more about this fellow named Lionel and what had really happened.

"I'm familiar with livestock. Mostly horses."

Jacob stepped into the stirrup and settled heavily upon his saddle. "Come by the house later today if you want the job. The ranch is about five miles north of here along this trail. You can't miss the place."

"I'll do that."

"And if your friend inside wants work, bring him along—the Irishman, not the Indian." Jacob and Casey rode down to help the others herd the horses onto the trail. In a few minutes they had taken the horses and were gone. Keane went back inside the cabin to tell them his plan.

Chapter Six

The heat of the day was upon the land when Keane and O'Brian rode under the shingle into the Lazy J compound and turned their horses toward the hitching rail in front of John Jacob's big, native-stone ranch house.

"Nice place," O'Brian commented, looking at the huge barn, a long, low bunkhouse, and the corrals that snaked away down into a grassy meadow. The Irishman nodded approvingly as he absentmindedly scratched at his beard and the old brand on his cheek.

Keane turned his reins around the rail and stepped up to the long porch. The door opened and a woman suddenly appeared there. She was tall and pretty, wearing a green linen taffeta dress that appeared out of place, considering the setting.

"Yes? What do you want?" she asked tersely.

"We've come to see Mr. Jacob."

"Why? So you can ask my husband more of your

questions? He already told Sheriff Hodgeback all he knows. We really don't need to be bothered anymore. You have the guilty man in custody. Do what you have to with him."

Keane glanced at O'Brian. The Irishman was grinning, seeing the mistake. Keane said, "We're not here about that, ma'am. Fact is, your husband invited us over. Seems he's short a couple wranglers."

"Oh." Her hostility instantly vanished. "I see. Well, John is not here. You will probably find him down behind the barn. They just brought in those green-broke horses and are getting them trail ready." She waved a hand vaguely in the direction of the barn.

"Thank you, ma'am. We'll find him." Keane and O'Brian left their horses there and started for the barn.

"See the way she was looking at you?" O'Brian said, once out of earshot.

"You mean like a bull eyeing the matador? She surely did seem upset about something."

"No, no, afterwards, when you told her why we was here."

Keane gave him a skeptical glance. "You and Ridere are surely cut from the same bolt. You two only have one thing on your minds."

O'Brian chuckled. "Me and Harry, we understand the finer pleasures of life."

"You two are going to end up on the wrong end of a smoking gun if you aren't careful."

The sound of voices reached them from beyond the barn. There was some cheering, followed almost at once by a collective groan. Keane and O'Brian came around the corner just as a wrangler was picking himself off the ground and brushing the dust from his chaps. He stalked back toward a mustang there. The horse was a claybank stallion standing about sixteen hands. At the moment he was snubbed down to a post and held there by a man pulling hard on the end of a rope. The horse rolled his big eyes warily at the man trying for the stirrup. Just as he was about to get a boot in it, the horse sidestepped skittishly. A couple of the wranglers standing outside the rails laughed. The man cursed the animal and tried again.

John Jacob was standing there, leaning on a rail and grinning with the others. Casey Owen was there too, and he recognized a couple of the riders who had showed up at the cabin earlier.

"I was wondering if you were going to take up the offer, Mr. Keane," Jacob said when Keane folded an arm across one of the rails beside the heavyset man.

"Breaking them to bit and saddle?"

"Lionel was supposed to gentle them some before we got our hands on them, but these that we brought in seemed to have more spunk in them than usual."

"Give me a horse with spunk any day over a spirit-broke nag. That's a good-looking animal."

Jacob laughed. "You know about horses? Yes, that's right, you said you did."

"Twenty years in the army, and a few years with the cavalry teaches a man a thing or two about livestock."

"The army? Retired, did you?"

Keane had retired, but it hadn't been his decision. General Crook had given him the choice. Face a court-martial, or turn in his resignation and keep his army pension. Well, at least Crook had put the matter in his hands. Friendship, it seemed, did account for something. "I retired," he answered briefly and let the matter drop.

The wrangler in the corral caught the stirrup and swung up onto the mustang. The man holding the snubbing rope let go and dove for safety behind the railings. Out in the middle of the corral there was something like a sudden four-legged explosion and the horse was airborne, legs stiff as fence posts. He bucked and whirled and did a couple more stiff-legged leaps, throwing the man on his back up and down upon the saddle like a pile driver. The wrangler lasted no more than ten seconds before sailing off. He picked himself off the ground, rescued his hat from the pounding hooves and limped out of the corral, massaging his hip as he left the arena.

"Think we ought to name that one Diablo," he noted, folding himself through the rails.

Jacob laughed and glanced at O'Brian. "Care to give him a try?"

Dougal O'Brian shook his head. "No, sir. At my age I'm liable to break something."

Jacob looked at Keane. "How about you? Every one of my boys have had a go at that one and he's sent them all flying. 'Course, no one would blame you if you backed out. Your friend has the right idea. There's no profit in busting yourself up just because you don't want to look bad in the eyes of my boys, here."

Keane grinned. He'd been thrown a challenge by this man and now everyone was watching him to see what he would do about it. Keane watched the mustang trotting in a circle at the far end of the corral. All at once the horse came to a stop and looked at him. Its nostrils flared as it breathed hard and its pale yellow coat was slick with sweat. Keane saw the faint quiver in its legs. The horse was tired, but its spirit was still unbroken.

"Every one of your men?" Keane asked, eyeing the seven of them standing there.

"Every one, and some more than once."

This mustang had been ridden more than seven

times. Keane did not have Royden Louvel's talent for figuring the odds, but he suspected the horse was near to giving in on the matter of allowing a man on his back. If not . . . well, Keane had been thrown from horses before. They were all watching him. Keane had once been a leader of men and you could not accomplish that without a sharp understanding of why men do what they do, and how to motivate them to do what you want them to do. Mere rank was not enough for some men. Some men put stock in things such as riding a horse, or taking a challenge. It was a sure way to get yourself accepted by them, and Keane would need their confidence if he was going to learn anything that might help him find Egan Driscoll's killer.

"All right. I'll give him a try."

Jacob's carefully groomed beard stretched across his face. "Lomis, go snub that mustang for Mr. Keane."

"That won't be necessary," Keane said, slipping through the rails and straightening on the other side. He eyed the horse and the horse eyed him right back. Speaking gently, he walked up to the wary animal, slowly reached for the snubbing rope and lifted it off its head.

"There you go. We won't be needing this any more, will we?" he soothed. The horse flinched away from his hand, but then permitted him to lightly stroke his neck. The stallion held Keane in his wary stare, looking as if he might explode in a fury of slashing hooves at any moment. But he didn't. Keane slowly took up the reins that dangled on the ground and laid them across the sleek neck.

"I'm going to get on your back now," he whispered near the mustang's ear, "and I'd appreciate it if you'd not make me look foolish in front of all these men. All right?"

Keane slowly lifted his boot to the stirrup. The horse rolled its big eyes. Keane put his weight to it and held the reins tight. He gave the mustang a moment to get used to the feel of it, then, clutching the saddle horn, he swung up onto its back.

The horse gave a leap, and then a whirl, but there was none of that stiff-legged pile driving as before. He bucked a couple of times, lifting Keane from the saddle, and then ran around the corral, driving Keane into the railings. But Keane held tight and fought the reins, turning the horse back toward the center. It leaped again and kicked its hind legs to the sky, nearly tossing Keane over its head. Keane stuck to the saddle. The horse tried ramming him into the snubbing post and dragging him along the rails again. And when that didn't work, the mustang simply resorted to running and kicking for a while. Then, as if suddenly deciding the effort wasn't worth it anymore, he settled down to a brisk lope around the corral.

Keane let the animal run a while, then pulled him to a stop in front of John Jacob. "There you go, Mr. Jacob. I broke him for you."

Jacob shook his head, a thin smiled fixed upon his face. "I reckon the army did teach you a thing or two about these animals."

"Reckon it did," Keane said, not letting on that Jacob's men had already done all the hard work for him, and that he suspected the mustang was ready to throw in the towel anyway.

"You want the job?"

"I'll work for you a while."

Jacob looked O'Brian up and down and said, "You look a mite long in the tooth for wrangling, but there are plenty of chores need doing. The lower corral needs mending, there are some stalls that need to be rebuilt and beavers have built a whole string of dams above us on this here creek where we take water for the house and animals. They have to be blown open. Know anything about dynamite, Mr. O'Brian?"

"Dynamite?" Dougal's eyes widened and gleamed with interest.

Keane said, "Fate has just brought you the right man, Mr. Jacob. O'Brian here is something of an expert with explosives."

"Are you, now?"

"Aye. Cut my teeth blowing bridges and cutting Yankee supply lines during the war. That was in the days before dynamite. Afterwards, I did a lot of work in the silver mines down in Mexico. I know dynamite about as good as I know anything."

"Well, then, it does look like fate has brought me the right man for the job." Jacob nodded his head, lightly stroking his short, neatly trimmed beard. "All right. You can have the job if you want it." He looked at Casey, who had been standing there listening all along. "Take these two to the bunkhouse and get them settled in, Casey. Then show Mr. O'Brian where we keep the dynamite."

He shifted his view back to the old Irishman. If he had noticed the *D* branded onto O'Brian's cheek, half hidden beneath the beard, he didn't mention it. "You can get started on those beaver dams first thing tomorrow."

Harrison Ridere grabbed the crutch Nantaje had fashioned for him from the branch of a cottonwood tree and stood, putting his weight on it. He tapped his way across the cabin and out into the soft light of late afternoon, peering hard at the line of trees down below. In places he could catch the glint of sunlight off moving water, but for the most part the stream was hidden from view.

A perfect place for an ambush, he thought, standing there looking for the Apache who had disappeared about an hour earlier.

Royden Louvel had ridden back into town. He had said he wanted keep to an eye on Lionel, but Ridere suspected that the Southerner was even more interested in rounding up a game of poker than in what was happening to the black man.

"Nantaje?" he called, his view shifting from the stream to the corrals and small barn. The quiet valley was peaceful, and Ridere was feeling a little better even though his leg was still useless and ached deep inside, like a worm was eating its way through it. But he was on the mend, he could feel it, and that in itself would make any day look brighter. The blue-and-white flash of a magpie swooped past him. The big bird landed atop a corral railing, then glided to the ground and started strutting and pecking at something.

Ridere called again for his friend, staring at the trees below where he had last seen the Indian. Turning back toward the cabin, he spied the Apache coming down from the ridge a few hundred yards beyond the barn. He was moving slowly, his eyes turned down to the ground, carefully scanning it as he came.

"Where did you go?" Ridere asked when Nantaje came back to the cabin.

Nantaje opened his fist and showed him a brass cartridge. "Found this over there," he said, nodding at the cottonwoods. "Followed some tracks up the stream to where a horse was waiting. Rider went off one way, then circled around and headed back another way. I followed them about a mile until I was sure he headed back toward the ranch."

"Driscoll's murderer *was* someone from the Lazy J."

"It seems that is so."

Ridere turned the cartridge over and read the head stamp. "Thirty-eight WCF."

Nantaje nodded. "A common enough caliber. I would make a guess that half the Winchesters around are chambered for the Thirty-eight Winchester Center Fire."

"And you would be right. I saw Lionel's rifle, and it's a Forty-four–Forty."

"That will make a big difference. Maybe it is time you go talk to Sheriff Hodgeback?"

Just the thought of facing Walter Hodgeback was like a cold finger dragging up his spine. "I'm not ready for that—not yet, at least."

"You would let them hang this man?"

"They can't hang Lionel. He's innocent. I'm sure any jury would see that and let him off."

"You speak of white man's justice?" Nantaje asked with a hint of mockery in his voice.

Ridere grimaced. "I know what you are thinking. Mind if I hold on to this for a little while?"

"You keep it."

Ridere took the cartridge inside with him. As he lay back on the bed, he turned it over, studying it. He had been trained in artillery before deserting the army and was something of an expert where small arms were concerned. Something about this particular cartridge caught his eye now, but whether or not it was important, he didn't know.

Chapter Seven

Sheriff Hodgeback came in off the street, leaving the door standing open to the faint breeze. He tossed his hat onto a chair and strode to his desk.

Lionel stood up from the edge of the cot where he had been sitting and grabbed an iron bar in each hand, glaring through them. "How long yo' gonna keep me locked up here, Sheriff?"

Hodgeback settled behind a cluttered desk and began shoving aside the papers to make room for the handful of envelopes he'd brought with him. He glanced across the small room at Lionel and laughed. "Now, that's a pretty stupid question, boy. You'll stay locked up inside that jail until a jury says otherwise. Then you'll be marched out back to the gallows where we'll stretch that black neck of yours."

"Ain't I s'pose to be innocent until proved otherwise?"

Hodgeback stopped grinning. "Not when you go and murder a white man, boy."

"I didn't kill Driscoll! How many times I gotta say dat to yo'?"

"The evidence calls you a liar. Two men heard your fight with Mr. Driscoll. They heard the gunshot, and when they reached the scene of the killing, you were standing over the body holding a rifle. I say that makes you guilty of murder. How dumb do you think we are, boy?"

"I already told yo'. Dat shot, it come from down by de stream."

"Hu-huh. And pigs fly." Hodgeback gave a short laugh. "You're going to swing for this, so better get used to the idea. Oh, by the way, I just talked to Judge Canaby. The trial is set for the day after tomorrow. He don't let no grass grow under his feet. It'll be in the morning, and if I know Canaby, you'll be stretching a new rope come sundown."

Lionel's fists tightened around the cold, black bars, straining at them helplessly, then he spun away and stalked the tiny cell like a caged panther. A sudden suffocating desperation had begun to return to him. It was an old feeling, one that had been buried and nearly forgotten over twenty years. He'd escaped slavery a half dozen times, only to be caught and returned to his master—to be bucked and whipped one more time. He was determined to try it again now . . . but how? Then a thought occurred to him. He spun around and clutched the bars again.

"Don't yo' at least got to get me a lawyer?" he asked. "Ain't dat something I deserve?"

Hodgeback raised his eyes from the letter he was reading. "A lawyer? You?" He laughed. "What man would defend you in a court of law?"

He was right. What man would defend him? Lionel went back to the cot and sat down, forearms upon his knees, his head drooping.

"But the county will appoint someone to represent you. It's the law, you know," Hodgeback told him. "These kinds of trials got to be done strictly according to the law."

A big beetle was working its way across the floor between Lionel's feet. He watched it find a crumb of bread and stop and begin to devour it. He was about to crush the insect beneath the heel of his boot when he stopped and just sat there, watching the little black creature working at the crumb, completely unaware that death was only a footstep away.

He had a thought and suddenly grinned. What would Miss Jacob have thought? Miss Jacob would have bust a gut if she'd seen him about to crush that critter. Rachel Jacob was about the most gentlest woman he'd ever know—besides his own mama. She was crazy for little helpless critters . . . and maybe he was just a little crazy too, thinking he could ever get a fair shake in this world.

John Russell Keane looked at the bunk Casey had pointed him toward. He tested the mattress with a hand and dropped his saddlebags and rifle onto it.

O'Brian took a bunk across the room and bounced on it a couple of times. "Beats sleeping on the ground any day, John." He lay back and stretched out his legs.

Casey said, "You two get settled in here. In the morning you can help with the horses, Keane." He introduced them to a couple of hands who were there. One man was reading a dog-eared copy of a stock newspaper. He said a brief howdy and went back to his reading. A second wrangler, building a fire in a small iron stove, said, "There'll be coffee ready in a little while."

"This ain't a big operation and you've already met most of the men," Casey said. "It's getting late and the rest of the boys should be coming back soon. We've got a couple of men minding the line shacks. You'll get to meet them later."

"Looks comfortable enough," Keane said, glancing down the long building to where perhaps two dozen bunks ranged along the walls.

"Mr. Jacob believes in taking care of his men. This is a good outfit to work for . . . now," he added, as if as an afterthought.

"Now?" Keane repeated.

Andy Garwood was the name of the man at the stove. He glanced up and said, "Now that that sonuvabitch Driscoll ain't here no more."

"Amen to that," the fellow behind the paper mumbled.

Casey struggled to keep from grinning.

Keane said, "Doesn't sound like Mr. Driscoll will be much missed."

"No, not by many on the Lazy J," Casey allowed.

"Why is that?"

"The man was an arrogant, whip-snapping ramrod, he was," Andy Garwood said. "I say Lionel deserves a medal for plugging the sonuvabitch, instead of sitting in jail. Lionel is a decent sort, even though he has his peculiarities, especially when it comes to tending them horses. But then, there ain't a man on the Lazy J that don't have some quirks, except maybe Corey Lomis. Corey is a straight-arrow fellow who never once crossed Driscoll." Garwood gave a laugh and said, "Probably half the men who worked for Driscoll had thought about putting a bullet in him. I even wish I had done it."

Keane looked at Casey. "Is that true?"

"True enough."

"Then anyone might have killed him."

"Except that there are two witnesses who saw Lionel do it," Casey said.

"That ain't exactly true," the man reading said, not bothering to lower his paper. "Way I got the story, they only heard the shot. When they come around the side of Lionel's cabin, that's when they saw him with his rifle."

"Maybe that is true, but he done it just the same," Casey said. He turned toward O'Brian. "Come with me and I'll show you where we keep the dynamite."

When they had gone, Keane sat on his bunk, looking around the place.

"Coffee's beginning to boil," Garwood said, putting his nose near a dingy windowpane and watching the long shadows that had moved across the yard.

"Sounds to me like no one here much cared about your murdered foreman." Keane said it casually. He did not want either of them to think he was particularly interested or fishing for information.

The newspaper rustled as the man turned a page. "That ain't exactly true either. There just might be one. Way I hear it, and mind you it's only rumor, some say the boss's wife and Driscoll they was—" He paused and lowered the paper, a sly grin to his face. "They was carrying on some, if you get my drift."

Garwood chuckled, shaking his head. He turned back to the stove, but he didn't say a word.

Keane whistled softly. "That's one way for a man to get himself shot." He was thinking of Ridere's seduction of the sheriff's wife, and wondered why some men chose to play such dangerous games.

With the men finishing up the day's work, John Jacob left the corral full of half-broken mustangs and strode back to the big stone house crouched among the trees, apart from the other ranch buildings. As he angled toward the front porch he caught a glimpse of his daughter sitting in a chair at the back of the house. Rachel appeared somber, frowning. Jacob stopped and stood there. A pair of mountain jays were hopping along the ground near her feet, begging for a scrap of food in their scolding, obnoxious way. But Rachel seemed not to notice them, and he wondered if he should go to her. Something was troubling Rachel, and that troubled him. Was it the murder of Egan Driscoll that had gotten to her, or maybe it was the departure of Peter Blake . . . or something else entirely? Rachel had always been a moody girl, and there was no telling what had grabbed hold of her now.

In the end, John Jacob decided to leave his daughter alone with her thoughts. He stepped up to the porch and opened the screen door, thinking he ought to put a couple of drops of oil on those squeaking hinges.

"Felicity?" he called from the parlor, peering first toward the doorway into the kitchen, then up the stairs to the second floor, where their bedroom was located.

"Felicity?"

"What do you want?" came his wife's sharp retort down the hallway. Her sewing room was just past his office and the door was open. Her voice told him that she was upset again. Experience instantly warned him to tread lightly. He sighed and started down the hallway. Both mother and daughter were in evil moods.

How simple life had been before females had entered it to complicate things.

John Jacob was an evenhanded man when it came to his women, and sometimes the best thing to do was to stand back and let the storm blow over. It always did. Frowning, he stepped through the door. Felicity was standing by the window, arms folded tightly, her back to him. She didn't turn when he entered the room.

"This whole affair has gotten you upset too, hasn't it?" he said gently. When Felicity didn't answer Jacob went on, "Well, at least we have the man who did it." He shook his head. "Never would have expected it of Lionel, though."

She turned slowly and peered at him. "You really think he did it?"

"Who else could have?"

Her eyes narrowed. He couldn't read what they were showing him. "Yes," she said suspiciously, "who else?" Felicity went back to staring out the window. There was nothing out there—nothing he could see from the doorway, at least.

"I'm going away, John," she said suddenly.

Her words shocked him. For a moment he had no reply. "Away? What are you saying?"

"I've just got to get away from here, that's all."

"From here or from me?"

She wheeled around, her skirt rasping across the floor. "From you, from this place, from this brutal land where men die and life just goes on as if nothing ever happened. And I want to take Rachel with me."

"Rachel?"

"She is such a sensitive girl. Egan's murder has gotten to her, or haven't you noticed? She can hardly speak without tears coming to her eyes. I have to get her away from here."

"I won't let you take Rachel!"

"You won't let me? No, of course not. You'd rather keep her here with all these . . . these boorish men. Do you know what they are doing? They are practically celebrating. They hated Egan. Every one of them. They are glad he's dead."

"Egan? That's the second time you used his first name. It has always been Mr. Driscoll before."

Felicity stiffened and her voice went suddenly flat. "I want to visit my sister in St. Louis, John. As soon as I can make the arrangements we are leaving." She whisked past him and started for the staircase.

"How far had it gone between you and Driscoll?" he asked coolly.

Felicity stopped at the foot of the stairs, a hand upon the turned balustrade. She looked at him, her face suddenly drained of color. "You knew?"

"I suspected."

"How long?"

"I'd wanted Casey to be foreman all along, but when you swayed me to making Driscoll foreman I had to ask myself why. There were lots of reasons, of course, but the one that stuck was the one I wanted to believe least of all. After that I kept my eyes open, and my ears."

His words stunned her into silence. Then Felicity gathered up her skirt in one hand and hurried up the stairs and through a doorway, shutting the door behind her.

John Jacob's heart was a stone in his chest. He drew in a breath and shook his head as he let it out and went into his office. He needed to be alone, to try to think this through. He loved Felicity and didn't want to lose her. But what could he do to keep her now? She wanted to leave, and she wanted to take Rachel with her. Jacob saw his world tearing apart before his eyes. Why did she feel she had to leave?

He didn't understand all that was happening. So much so soon. Driscoll murdered on his land, Lionel in jail, Felicity leaving him and Rachel's sudden gloom, moping around like a lost puppy. What was he to do?

Jacob crossed to his desk and lowered himself wearily into the chair. His eyes traveled around the room, not really seeing the familiar surroundings. But then something caught his attention. He stared at his Winchester, resting in the gun rack upon the wall. Above it was his shotgun, and below an old Sharps Buffalo gun he never used anymore.

Jacob sat there looking at the rifle. Something was wrong, but he couldn't quite put a finger on what it was. It was exactly where it belonged, yet something . . .

Then he remembered. He had just cleaned the rifle. Had finished the job while Driscoll had been in the office. He'd walked the man out, leaving the rifle leaning against the wall near the door. Jacob frowned and tried to think back. He couldn't remember ever putting the rifle up. That was odd. No one ever entered the office. It was his private domain, unlike the rest of the house, which was Felicity's concern. This one room was off limits to the fussing of his wife. He thought it odd that he couldn't remember returning the rifle to its proper place. Could Felicity have put it away? He supposed it was possible, even likely.

John Jacob dismissed the puzzle, returning his thoughts to Felicity's announcement and the gut-wrenching truth finally out in the open. Suddenly his eyelids compressed. Jacob pushed back the chair and went to the gun rack, lifting the Winchester and levering open the breech bolt. The glint of brass caught the sunlight through the window as a cartridge cartwheeled through the air and clattered upon the wood floor.

Jacob picked up the bullet and stared at it, then at the rifle. He'd cleaned the rifle and loaded the magazine tube, but he had not chambered a cartridge. He was certain of that. He never kept a cartridge chambered in the rifle when it was in the house. Jacob put his nose to the chamber and smelled the acrid odor of gunpowder. He slipped a piece of white paper in the open breech to reflect sunlight up the barrel and peered down the muzzle. The barrel was dirty. The rifle had been fired.

Jacob put the rifle back on the gun rack. He stood there pondering it, then looked out the door. Beyond it lay the hallway and then the parlor. Someone had entered his house, had taken the rifle, had used it and then had returned it to the rack—its usual place.

That someone had to have known where the *usual* place for the gun was, or they'd have returned it to where they had found it. Most of the men on the ranch had been in the office at one time or another. Any one of them could have taken it, used it and then put it back in the gun rack.

But most of the men owned their own guns.

The question in Jacob's mind was, why use his?

He didn't have an answer to that—at least not yet.

Chapter Eight

The next morning Keane went off with the wranglers to bust broncs. While he and the other men were battering their backsides upon a breaking saddle, O'Brian loaded a packhorse with fifty pounds of dynamite from the powder magazine, and rode away to dismantle some beaver dams.

Throughout the morning Keane battled the half-broke mustangs, taking his turn at getting them used to saddle and bit. It was a brutal job, and every time he heard the distant boom of another beaver dam biting the dust, he remembered he was not as young as he once was. The way it all worked out, Dougal O'Brian was getting off easy with the job he had drawn. But then, O'Brian was twenty years older than he. Keane was glad the old Irishman didn't have to bust broncs, and that he was doing something he actually liked; something for which he had a special talent.

By noon they had finished and Keane was hobbling

like an old man, favoring his left hip. He dragged himself back to the bunkhouse with the others for their noonday meal and hopefully a few hours of rest to ease the soreness.

"Anyone notice how relaxed life has become now that Casey is the new foreman?" one of the men commented as he sopped up the juice from his baked beans with a piece of bread.

"Too bad someone didn't bushwhack Driscoll a long time ago." Hep Johnson laughed. "But I sure wish there was something we could do to help Lionel out of this fix he's got himself into."

"Lionel is getting just what he deserves," Corey Lomis said.

"Aw, you always did suck up to Driscoll. But it didn't get you nowhere, did it? He rode you just as hard as everyone else," Andy Garwood said.

"One thing for sure, no one is gonna miss his sharp tongue. I don't recall Driscoll ever once saying anything nice about anyone! The man was harder than nails and about as bitter as Indian squash growing in a manure pile," Johnson said.

Jake Laine, the lanky cowboy who had been reading the stock paper the evening before, was a quiet man who generally kept to himself. But Keane had noted that when he did make the effort to speak, his words bore listening to. "That ain't exactly true."

"Yeah? Who?" Elwell Farnham asked, just before filling his mouth with a piece of steak.

Laine shook his head and grinned. "You got to figure that out of the twenty or so people on the Lazy J, at least one of them must have had some feeling for Driscoll."

Farnham said, "Not on this ranch, not unless maybe Mr. Jacob might miss him. But not for long; he's got ten times the foreman in Casey than he ever had in Driscoll."

Keane was impressed by the total lack of remorse over the murder. It seemed every man there had thought about killing Driscoll at one time or another. The only regret he heard was that one or another of them hadn't been the one to pull the trigger. They lamented Lionel's predicament, but they cheered the man for having the guts to do it.

A little while later Ralph Weatherby came into the bunkhouse carrying a saddlebag over his shoulder. He noticed Keane right off and came over and introduced himself. Afterwards, he took what was left of the food and told them word of the murder had reached the line shack already, and that he had hightailed it back down off of Castle Mountain to see if it was true. The men rehashed the event for Weatherby, spicing it up some as men tend to do when they sink their teeth into really good stories.

Weatherby listened with a frowning face, but the festive atmosphere around the table was infectious and he was grinning with the rest of them by the time everyone had finished adding their own details and opinions.

Keane wondered about a man who could be so thoroughly hated as Egan Driscoll had been. Certainly the man must have had some redeeming traits? Keane let his thoughts drift back to an earlier time, recalling the men he had commanded as an officer in the army. He'd known more than a few who had been hard to get along with, but not one of them had been as bad as Driscoll—or as bad as the men who had worked for him made him out to be.

Casey came in a few minutes later and spent some time bantering with the men as he filled a tin cup with

coffee. It was plain everyone liked him. And it was just
as plain that Casey was feeling large and full of life,
and Keane suspected Driscoll's death and Casey's sub-
sequent promotion to foreman had much to do with
that.

Casey drifted over to where Keane was sitting and
asked how he was feeling. He had a friendly way
about him, and Keane could see how the men might
like him.

"Kinda sore on the south forty," Keane replied, grinning.

"Thought so. I saw how you walked when you left
the corral." He laughed. "You'll get used to it." He
announced that he needed a couple of men to ride with
him out to the pinery sawmill to bring back a load of
boards for the corrals. He had his volunteers almost at
once, and told the rest of the men they could kick back
for the afternoon and rest their behinds.

"Now there is a foreman who knows how to treat his
men," Hep Johnson declared when Casey had gone.

Yep, Keane thought, *Casey Owen knows how to han-
dle men.*

Keane went to the window and watched the men
head for the barn. A few minutes later a big freight
wagon pulled by four horses lumbered out. Casey was
at the reins, and a man rode beside him on the seat
while a third lounged in the empty bed. The wagon
rumbled past the bunkhouse, then swung out onto the
road that led away from the Lazy J headquarters.

Keane was restless with time on his hands. There was
a dog-eared copy of *Harper's Weekly* that he thumbed
through for a while, but spending an afternoon doing
nothing was not Keane's way, especially when he had
things on his mind. He wondered how Harrison Ridere

was mending from his snakebite, and he knew Lionel's time was running out. He couldn't afford to lie about the bunkhouse doing nothing.

He grabbed up his rifle and slipped his gun and gunbelt over his shoulder. The air outside was pleasantly warm, sweetly scented with the pine from the forested hillsides that hemmed in the pretty valley where John Jacob had located his ranch. The buildings rested in a bowl of about two hundred acres, rimmed by green forests and decorated with startling wind-sculpted sandstone, as if nature had purposely carved and placed each and every one of them. Beyond the hills Keane could see the taller peaks of the San Juan Mountains. The stream that flowed past was clear and cold, fed by the winter snow packs that lasted on the northern slopes long into summer.

As he started for the stone house among the mulberry trees he heard a far-off boom roll down the valley. Dougal O'Brian was still at work. That cold stream that flowed past the house and made a sweep toward the corrals seemed to be moving a bit faster than Keane remembered. O'Brian was making headway on those beaver dams.

Keane saw the girl sitting in a chair behind the house. He'd heard that John Jacob had a daughter, and he bent his steps around one of the huge trees to say hello. His heavy footsteps startled her. She came around suddenly in the chair.

"Good afternoon, ma'am," he said.

The girl brushed at her eye and instantly composed herself. "Oh. You must be one of the new men Father hired."

"John Russell Keane is the name," he said, smiling. "I'm sorry if I startled you. I was on my way to talk to your father and saw you sitting here. Thought I'd introduce myself. You must be Rachel."

The girl managed a halfhearted smile. "You didn't startle me, Mr. Keane. I was just thinking, that's all."

"You appeared pretty deep in thought. Good thing I wasn't an Apache."

Her grin widened out some into a smile. "There aren't any Apaches hereabouts, Mr. Keane."

"Well, then how about a Ute?"

"We have a few of those," she allowed. Rachel Jacob had a funny way of smiling; kind of crooked and squinty. It wasn't real pretty, but there was something infectious and honest in it, and Keane took a liking to the girl right off. There was a small sack of grain on the ground by the side of her chair and a bowl of peanuts upon her lap. Nearby, three squirrels were tearing into brown husks with their sharp teeth. A mountain jay winged to a branch nearby and scolded him.

"Looks like someone else is vying for your attention," he said.

"Never mind him. I call him Mr. Greedy. All he does is takes the peanuts away and hide them. He doesn't even eat them and he never seems to get enough." Rachel tossed another peanut to the ground. The jay swooped down, hopped over to it and swallowed it whole into a pouch in its neck, looking like it had suddenly developed a goiter. She threw out another and he gobbled it down too, then flew off to another tree a few hundred feet away.

"See what I mean? He doesn't eat them. He just carries them off and hides them."

"Saving for a rainy day?"

"I reckon," Rachel said. Then her voice turned somber and she looked away.

"Is your father inside?"

"Yes, I think so."

"I'll just go see him, then."

"Nice meeting you, Mr. Keane."

"You too, ma'am."

At the front he rapped on the door and waited. It opened a few moments later. John Jacob was standing there.

"Mr. Keane? What can I do for you?" Jacob's manner was abrupt and Keane knew he had caught him at a bad moment.

"I can come back later, if you like."

"No, no, that won't be necessary." Jacob frowned. "Now or later, it's all the same. Come in." He led the way across the parlor, down a hall and into a room with a window that looked out onto the side yard with a glimpse of the back. Keane could just see Rachel from here, tossing out a handful of grain to a flock of birds pecking at the ground.

Jacob's office was cluttered but comfortable, reflecting the wants and pleasures of a man. It smelled pleasantly of tobacco, wood and leather. The heads of a mounted elk and a bighorn sheep decorated the walls, and a tall clock ticked lazily in one corner. A coat rack holding an assortment of hats and jackets stood in another. There was a stone fireplace faced by two rawhide chairs, and nearby there was a rifle rack holding a long Sharps rifle, a Winchester carbine and a shotgun. A portrait of himself and his wife occupied a place on a wall next to various paintings of landscape and wildlife. There were some framed photographs too, of Jacob as a younger man and other people. Probably family members, Keane decided.

Jacob went around behind a desk that occupied much of the floor in front of the window and lifted the lid of a cigar box. "Care for a cigar?" he asked, taking one for himself and offering another to Keane.

Keane took the cigar and bent toward the match Jacob had scratched to life against a smooth, quartz paperweight. The rancher sat down and motioned Keane to one of the rawhide chairs.

"Sorry I was short just now. There is a lot going on, a lot on my mind, that is."

"Understood. Have you heard any more about the murder?"

Jacob shook his head, sucking deeply and rapidly at the cigar. "No, nothing more to hear. Lionel murdered Driscoll and now he'll pay the price."

"From what I have heard in the little time I've been here, no one actually saw the shooting."

"Saw it or not, he did it. No doubt about it. Lionel's good with horses, but he's never been very good around people. Why do you think he lives the way he does? He's a loner, and he likes it that way." Jacob drew in another lungful of smoke. "And frankly, Egan Driscoll was not very good with people either. I suppose you've heard already. He wasn't much liked by the men. My mistake. I should have made Casey foreman right from the start."

There was something eating at the man, something that went deeper than the murder of Egan Driscoll.

"Well, it'll all be over soon." Jacob's voice lowered and his view seemed to hover somewhere in the empty space between the ceiling and the floor. "And then maybe we can get back on with life as usual."

Jacob fell silent a moment, peering at the coil of smoke from the tip of his cigar. He suddenly drew in a sharp breath and looked at Keane. "What is it you wanted to see me about?"

"Casey says he has nothing for me to do the rest of

the day and I wanted to ride out and check up on my friend, if it's all right with you."

"The young fellow with the snakebite? Certainly. Go see your friend. Hope he is doing better."

"Nantaje knows how to treat snakebites. Harry is in good hands."

"Nantaje, that's the Injun. What are you men up to, riding with an Injun?"

"Nantaje used to be one of my scouts, when I was with General Crook, down in the Arizona Territory."

"That would make him an Apache."

"He is."

"How long were you in the army, Mr. Keane?"

"Almost twenty-five years."

"That's a long time. Retired, did you?"

"Retired," he replied briefly, not wanting the inquiry to go any further. And to make sure it didn't, Keane stood and thanked Jacob for the cigar. "I'll be back later this evening."

John Jacob accompanied him through the parlor. Keane heard a sound from above and when he looked, Mrs. Jacob was standing at the head of the stairs, looking down at them.

"Ma'am," he said, touching the brim of his hat.

She did not reply, but turned away and went back through a doorway up there.

"The missus is not feeling well," Jacob offered as an explanation for her queer behavior. "Like the rest of us, she's upset over what has happened."

The two men went outside, and Keane was about to leave when a rider came loping up the road. He rode under the Lazy J shingle and up to the house. He was a young man, in his early twenties, slightly built, with a rash of freckles across his sunburned face. He reined to a halt and gave Keane a glance, then grinned and said to John Jacob, "I hear you got a new foreman, Mr. Jacob. I've come to see if I can have my old job back."

"I sorta figured you'd be back, Peter." He introduced Peter Blake to Keane, then told Blake to go claim a bunk for himself. "Casey will be pleased to see you back."

"When I heard Driscoll went and got himself killed, I just knew Casey would get the job." Blake's smile faded and he said, "I talked with Lionel a while before I left."

Jacob looked pained. "How is he holding up?"

Blake frowned. "Not too good. You know Lionel, he put stock in freedom. Being locked up for him is like hobbling one of his mustangs. He's plum unhappy and looking real down. He keeps insisting he's innocent. And I believe him."

"He's not," Jacob said firmly. "I hate to see a man like Lionel swing, but he did it."

"Well, Judge Canaby is getting a jury together. Gonna have the trial real soon, I hear." Blake shook his head, his voice taking on a somber tone. "Sure wish there was something I could do to help him. I'd bust him out of there if I thought I could get away with it."

"Just leave things as they are, Peter. No sense risking your neck to protect a murderer, no matter how your heart tells you otherwise."

Blake's frown deepened. "Thanks for my job back. I'll go get squared away now." The young man turned his horse toward the bunkhouse.

Keane left Jacob standing there and strode across the yard. At the corner of the barn he turned back and saw Blake's horse among the mulberry trees behind the ranch house. He took a few steps to one side and spied them together. Rachel's face was beaming, and Blake was smiling too. They spoke a few minutes, then strolled off together, each keeping a discreet distance from the other. It was that awkward shyness that often comes between a man and a woman in the early stages of courtship. Keane grinned, understanding suddenly why Blake had been so eager to get his old job back.

They disappeared into the stand of trees along the stream that flowed past the house, and when they had gone, Keane went around back to the corral, cut his horse from the others, saddled it and rode away.

Chapter Nine

John Keane took the trail south, and once the buildings of the Lazy J had dropped from sight, he settled down to do some thinking, letting his horse amble at its own pace. He was in no hurry. The afternoon was still early and the countryside he was riding through pleasing to the eye. It was the high desert mountain country of southern Colorado, mostly scattered pine and scrub oak. Lower, in the canyons that cut up the land, the heat would be oppressive this time of year, but at this elevation, with a mild breeze out of the north, it was downright relaxing, especially because the gentle gait of his animal was nothing at all like the rollicking broncs he had ridden that morning.

He mulled over just what he and O'Brian had managed to accomplish, which was exactly nothing. What he had thought would be an easy job was suddenly turning into a puzzle. Keane had expected to find men on both sides of the fence where Egan Driscoll was concerned. Instead, he had discovered that every one of them had hated the man equally. Anyone could have been the murderer. Not that he had detected a killer instinct in any man he'd met so far. But then, the real killer would be wary not to let that show.

He'd been told it was Hep Johnson and Corey Lomis who had been with Driscoll the evening he was killed. They were the ones who had brought Lionel back to the ranch, where he'd been held until Sheriff Hodgeback could be contacted. That pretty much ruled them out.

Keane had to wonder why he had allowed himself to be dragged into this in the first place. It was because of Harry, and his indiscretions with the sheriff's wife, that they were involved at all now. Keane was of a mind to haul Harry into town to tell his story and be done with the matter. But then the real murderer would still be loose. The thought of not trying to find him out rankled Keane's sense of justice. No, he'd see this through—at least a little while longer.

He considered the men he had met. Most were on the ranch when Driscoll had been shot. Ralph Weatherby had been away, taking a message to the line shack on Castle Mountain. Who else, he wondered, could have had the opportunity to bushwhack the foreman? The rumor about Driscoll and John Jacob's wife, if true, would be just one more motivation to kill the man. Maybe it hadn't been anyone from the ranch at all. An old enemy, perhaps? Keane wondered. From what he'd heard about Egan Driscoll, he'd not be surprised if there wasn't a line of past enemies stretching clear to Kansas City.

Keane frowned and shook the puzzle from his head. His thoughts drifted to California. He'd heard there was prime farming land out on the coast, and right now a little place near the ocean sounded pretty good to him.

The cabin appeared ahead, sitting beyond a string of mostly empty corrals. Ridere's horse was there, and so was Nantaje's. But Royden Louvel's mount was gone.

When Keane rode up, Nantaje stepped out of the cabin to meet him. "How's he doing?" Keane asked.

"I'm doing better, John," Ridere called from inside.

Nantaje nodded. "Harry not going to walk swiftly for a while, but the swelling has stopped. He will still be hobbling for some weeks."

Keane turned his horse loose in the corral.

"You walk like you hurt," Nantaje observed when he came back.

"Been busting broncs. That was supposed to be Lionel's job." Inside the cabin he found Harrison Ridere propped up on the bed with a pillow against the wall.

"Well, what have you learned?" Ridere asked.

Keane gave a short laugh. "Only that Egan Driscoll was a son of a bitch, to use their words, and hated by just about everyone on the ranch."

"Then maybe he deserved what he got."

"That seems to be the sentiment around the bunkhouse at the Lazy J."

"So, where does that leave Lionel?" Ridere asked.

"Still in jail and looking at a rope. Heard they were getting a jury together for a trial. Where is Louvel?"

"He went back to town," Nantaje said. "Said he wanted to keep an eye on how things were going there."

"Most likely looking for a game of poker," Ridere put in.

"I wouldn't be selling Louvel short," Keane said.

Ridere gave a short laugh. "That's strange coming from you, a 'damned Yankee.'"

Keane grinned. Although Royden Louvel never let him forget they had both fought on the opposite sides of the Mason-Dixon line, the two had more in common than Louvel would ever have wanted to admit.

Ridere took a spent cartridge from his pocket and gave it to Keane. "Nantaje found this down by the stream."

"Thirty-eight WCF," Keane noted, turning the shell over and reading the head stamp.

"That's what killed Driscoll."

"Not much to go on," Keane said. "Not like there is only one gun that shoots a bullet like this. Plenty of rifles and revolvers chambered for the Thirty-eight–Forty."

"Ah, but there's where you are wrong."

Keane raised a questioning eyebrow.

"Look at it again."

"What am I looking for?"

"See that line on the back of the shell?"

Keane turned it toward the window, and when he had angled it just so, he saw what Ridere was referring to.

"It was made when the cartridge was fired. The bolt face of the rifle that fired that round will have a deep scratch in it. A scratch that will match the line on that shell exactly."

"Hmm."

"And it *was* fired from a rifle," Ridere went on. "The extractor marks are plain enough on the rim."

"I see them."

"There is something else I want to show you, John Russell," Nantaje said.

Keane followed the Apache down to the stream where they hunkered over some tracks. "The killer waited here. Much hard ground. He left no clear footprints, but you can see where the dry grass is broken over here, and here. His horse was tied a few hundred feet away, out of sight."

From this vantage point, Keane had a clear line of sight to the cabin, but because of the trees and boulders, the murderer would have been difficult if not impossible to spot. "Whoever he was, he picked a good spot to set up an ambush."

"Come look at this." Nantaje started along a rocky shelf around the shoulder of a sandstone bluff and down a ravine. "The horse was tied here. The murderer rode off this way." Nantaje bent over a track and traced it with a finger. "His horse has a problem. See, left front hoof is narrower than the others."

Keane saw it clearly, now that Nantaje had pointed it out to him.

"Another thing: The murderer—he rode away to the east, but then circled back and headed straight for the ranch."

"Hmm. He's trying to throw off anyone who might have discovered his tracks."

"Looks like it."

"And that means the murder must still be on Lazy J right now."

"That would be my guess, John Russell."

Keane took the spent cartridge from his pocket and considered it a moment. "Well, that narrows it some. All I have to do is find a rifle with a marred bolt face, and a horse with one hoof slightly narrower than the others."

"Tie them both to a man, and you have the murderer."

95

"Pretty flimsy evidence to go on, if you ask me," Keane said.

Nantaje's face remained unmoved. "We can always head out to California, John Russell."

Keane grinned. "Yes, we can always do that." Then he narrowed a curious eye at the Apache. "Just why is it are you tagging along with us to California? I know what is drawing Ridere. It's all those pretty señoritas, and the Mexican border nearby just in case the army discovers he's a deserter. And O'Brian's reasons are pretty much the same, only he likes being down close to the border so he can skedaddle across whenever he gets to thinking about what the army did to him forty years ago."

"What about Louvel?"

Keane smiled as he shoved the cartridge back into his pocket and stood. "Mr. Louvel thinks San Francisco would be a profitable place to settle down for a while and play some cards. Then it's off to Australia for him. That should put him far enough away from the past he's been running from. But you, Nantaje? I don't know that you have ever said why you are going."

The Apache stood and brushed the dust from his hands against the worn blue cavalry trousers. "Then I will tell you, John Russell. It's the big water."

"The big water?"

"The Pacific Ocean. I've never seen water so wide that you can not look across to the other side. Or boats bigger than the barracks at Fort Bowie. O'Brian says it's so."

"It is."

"I want to see for myself."

Keane laughed. "A desert-born fellow like yourself going to see the 'big water.'"

"And why do you go?"

"Me?" Keane gave that a moment's thought. "I guess in some way it's like going back to my roots. I was born and raised on a farm. Been thinking lately that I'd like to get back to one someday, but I have no interest in going back east to do so. I hear there is a valley in California where a man can grow grapes enough to fill a small river with wine. Or grow practically anything else that he wanted to. I think maybe I'll try to find a farm, Nantaje. That's why I'm going to California."

The Apache shook his head. "You are not a farmer, John Russell."

"I'm not? Then what am I?"

"You are a warrior. On a farm you will feel trapped. Soon you will start to look for another war to fight. It might not be a war like the gray coats of the past, or the Apache, but you will find something, anything. You will always find the next battle to fight, John Russell. That is the way you are. That is why you will not leave now for California. This man Lionel, he needs your help, just like my people needed it down in Mexico. And the one who murdered Driscoll—he needs to be found. This is just another battle to you. Maybe not with soldiers and guns and war lances. But another battle just the same."

As they walked back to the cabin, John Keane knew that Nantaje was right.

It was after dark when Keane returned to the Lazy J. He put his horse in with the others in the common corral and carried his saddle into the barn. The big building was dark except for the faint flicker of lamp light coming from one of the far stalls. Keane put his gear away and strolled down the aisle where the family's personal mounts were kept and found Rachel Jacob sitting upon a stool, gently rubbing liniment into the foreleg of a tobino mare. She looked up at the sound of his footsteps.

"Nice looking horse," he said.

She smiled at him. "Hello, Mr. Keane. Yes, she is. Her name is Riata. Father gave her to me on my fifteenth birthday."

Keane nodded at the can of liniment. "Did Riata hurt herself?"

"Prairie dog hole last week. We both went down hard. I was all right, but thought at first she had broken her leg." Rachel frowned. "We'd of had to put her down if she had broken it. Fortunately, the leg was only bruised and badly sprained. But it will be a while before she can be ridden."

"I'm sure with you caring for her, she'll be spanking new in no time."

Rachel finished dressing the leg then closed up the can and wiped her hands upon a towel. Keane held the lantern for her as she put the liniment away in a cupboard. They left the barn and she pulled a knitted shawl over her shoulders, looking up at the stars. Slowly her smile faded and when she looked back at him there was sadness hidden there among the shadows of her face. Her view shifted to the stone house across the way.

"Why do people sometimes do the things they do, Mr. Keane?" she asked, looking out into the darkness.

"I suppose there are lots of reasons. Some do things out of their needs, others out of their wants." He paused, then added thoughtfully, "Out of disgrace or out of honor."

"What kind of needs or wants would make one person hurt another?"

"Well, sometimes when you're hurting real bad, you just want to strike out at whatever it is that's causing the pain. Afterwards, you realize the pain hasn't really gone away, only changed."

She looked at him. "So, what's the answer?"

"I don't have an answer for you, Rachel. It is something built into human nature, I reckon. Man seems to naturally do what he knows he shouldn't, and doesn't do what he knows he should. And I'm not wise enough to figure out why." He looked at her. "This got something to do with Lionel?"

She winced and turned away from him. "Partly. And partly with my father and mother, and partly with everyone on the ranch." She shivered and drew the shawl tighter.

He waited, but she had withdrawn into herself. Keane sensed there was more to this girl than just the quiet wallflower most of the men assumed her to be. She formed deep thoughts and she dwelled on them, turning them over and examining them from every side. Suddenly she drew in a sharp breath, as if coming out of a trance.

"Good night, Mr. Keane," she said.

"Good night, Miss Jacob."

Rachel started toward her home. He watched her go until the darkness beneath the spreading mulberry trees swallowed her up, then turned his steps toward the bunkhouse.

O'Brian was combing out the knots in his beard with his fingers while squinting at himself in a tin mirror on the wall when Keane came in from the night. "There you are," the Irishman said. "Where did you get off to?"

"Rode out to check up on Ridere."

Keane dropped his rifle and gunbelt on the bunk and poured himself a cup of coffee from the pot on the stove. There were a dozen men laying about, talking or occupying themselves mending tack, sharpening knives, reading dime novels. He did not know all the men by name yet, but they all knew his. Casey was sitting at the table with a couple of the boys, swapping stories. He glanced up and said, "How is your friend doing?"

"He's on the mend, but he'll be hobbling around on a crutch for the next few weeks."

"Glad to hear it," Casey said, turning back to his buddies. Casey was used to living with these men and seemed to enjoy their company. He had not yet gotten comfortable alone in the foreman's house that now rightfully was his to use.

Keane gave O'Brian a nod, went outside and sat on the top step of the porch. O'Brian followed him out the door and leaned on the railing. Beyond the ranch complex the land was velvet black and stars frosted the heavens.

"Did you learn anything?" Keane asked softly so his voice would not carry to the men inside bunkhouse.

"Beavers build mighty strong dams," O'Brian noted flatly.

The tall, ex-army major looked over and grinned. "And what about Driscoll?"

"Oh, he's the one you mean." O'Brian scratched at the scar beneath his beard. "Only that there ain't nobody hereabouts who seems particularly grieved over him being gone. But then, I haven't had much time to poke around, what with me spending all my time freighting dynamite from one beaver burg to the next, like I done all day."

Keane's view was fixed upon a rectangle of light from the window across the way where Jacob and his family lived. "Nantaje found some tracks down by the stream where the ambusher had lain in wait. And a spent cartridge from his rifle. It was a Thirty-eight–Forty."

O'Brian inclined his head at the bunkhouse door. "A couple rifles of that caliber inside there."

"I know. Need to get a closer look at them first chance I have to be alone."

"What's to look at?" O'Brian asked.

"The rifle that killed Driscoll left a mark on the shell. Ridere thinks there will be a matching mark on the bolt face of the killer's rifle."

They heard footsteps scrape the porch behind them. Young Peter Blake had just stepped out of the doorway and was standing there watching them. Blake drifted over and leaned against one of the posts.

"Catching some fresh air?" he asked, fishing tobacco and paper from a vest pocket and building himself a cigarette.

Was there a note of suspicion in the man's voice, or was it only Keane's imagination? He was about to tell O'Brian about the hoofprint Nantaje had found but now that could wait.

"I like to hear the crickets sing, and the sounds the horses make in their corral when they are bedding down for the night. It's real peaceful and reassuring."

"Reassuring?"

Keane laughed softly. "Comes from fighting the Apache, son, and wanting to keep my scalp in place."

"Heard you were in the army. Heard you're good at busting broncs, too."

"No better than any other man in the outfit."

Blake flicked his match into the darkness and leaned there, smoking, watching the house across the yard as Keane had been a few moments before. An uneasy silence settled over the men. Finally O'Brian stirred himself and said, "Think I'll go see an Indian about a blanket," and he clumped down the steps and wandered off toward the privy.

"Didn't I see you and Rachel coming from the barn a few minutes ago?" Blake asked.

So, that was what had been on the young man's mind. Although Blake managed to hide the emotion from his voice, Keane knew he was sweet on the girl. He smiled inwardly at the notion that Blake would consider him a threat where Rachel Jacob was concerned. "She was doctoring her horse," Keane answered.

"She seems . . . upset lately," Blake went on, still staring at the lighted window beyond the dark mulberry trees.

"A lot of that going around here. A lot to be upset over."

Blake looked over. "No one much cared for Driscoll. But just the same, a man doesn't deserve to be murdered just because he's hard on his men."

"I understand Driscoll ran you off the Lazy J the day he was murdered."

Blake stiffened slightly. "Yeah, he did. What interest do you have in it? You didn't know him, did you?"

"Never heard the name before yesterday."

"Well, him and me, we never did get along. Can't say as I'm any less sorry to see him dead than any other man here." Blake finished his smoke and ground the butt beneath his boot. "Your friend is coming back." Blake inclined his head at O'Brian, who was strolling in from the night, hitching a suspender over an arm. "I'll let you two get on with your talk," he said and went back inside the bunkhouse.

Chapter Ten

Keane was awake early, with the others, but no one was talking about the work that needed to be done. This day was to be different. Word had come down the evening before when the men had returned from the mill with the wagonload of lumber that Lionel's trial was set for later that morning, and that Hep Johnson and Corey Lomis were to be there as witnesses against the black man, they being the only two who had witnessed the whole thing.

From the front porch Keane watched Casey cross the few dozen yards from the foreman's cabin to the bunkhouse. Casey gave Keane a nod and said, "Breakfast about ready?"

"Just about." Keane lifted the tin cup he was holding. "Coffee is done."

They went inside, where Garwood was stirring up eggs in the big iron pan on the cook stove. The smell of brewed coffee filled the building, and the pleasing odor of scrambled eggs, fried bacon and griddle cakes had the men on pins and needles, fussing with their tin plates and silverware.

"Smells good 'nough to eat, Andy," Casey told Garwood.

"Grab yourself a plate, boss. It's just about done now."

The men all ate together at the long table, speaking of things that mattered to ranch hands, but mostly they talked of the upcoming trial. Keane kept quiet, listening to what was being said and all the while glancing at the bunks and scouting out which men owned rifles. Most of them did. There was a Remington, a Spencer, and a couple of Springfields among them . . . and four Winchesters. But Keane would have to wait until he was alone before examining them.

After breakfast Casey announced that Corey and Hep had to come into town with him, but anyone else who wanted to attend the trial could ride with them too. He wanted some of the men to remain behind because there were chores that had to get done regardless. Harvey Oldebrook, the farrier, said he had too many animals to get ready before the trail drive to go taking a day off.

Blake said he didn't care to see the spectacle and offered to stay as well. Keane had been looking for an opportunity to nose around, and with most of the men off attending the trial, this might be his only chance. He volunteered himself and O'Brian, and the rest of the men tossed their dirty plates into the washtub and ambled across to the barn to saddle up.

Keane watched them from the bunkhouse porch.

Nearly the whole ranch was going, with the exception of Mrs. Jacob and Rachel, who were not among the riders. Keane glanced over at Blake, wondering if his staying behind had anything to do with Rachel not going into town. Maybe they had planned it this way. He grinned, remembering how it was to be young and in love.

The riders assembled near John Jacob's house and waited for the owner to show up. Jacob rode from the barn and spoke a few moments to Casey, pointing toward the corrals. Casey nodded, then turned his horse toward the bunkhouse and rode over.

"While we are away I want you three to work on those corrals. The lumber I brought in last night is down there already, still in the wagon. Peter, you know where that extra keg of nails is in case you run short?"

"I know where it is," Blake replied.

"Replace whatever boards need replacing. There are some weak ones, and some about gnawed through. We'll be running cows into those pens next week and I don't want any of them busting through it."

"We'll work on it, Mr. Owen," Keane said.

"See you later this evening."

"Hope the trial goes well for Lionel," Keane added.

Casey frowned. "That's my wish too, but I don't give Lionel much of a chance. The evidence against him is pretty cut and dried." Casey reined his horse around and trotted back to the others, and the company of men rode off toward town.

When everyone had gone, Blake went back inside the bunkhouse.

O'Brian scratched at his beard and said in a low voice, "That fellow, Lionel, is running out of time. And we are still no closer to finding the real killer."

"One of us needs to take a look at those rifles inside the bunkhouse."

"Can't do it now, not with Pete and Harvey in there," O'Brian said. "I'll make some excuse to slip away from the work later."

Keane said, "Let's go take a look at that corral." They went down the steps to look over the job Casey had assigned to them. But suddenly Keane stopped.

"What is it?"

The ex-army major stood there staring down where Casey's horse had pawed the hard ground. The narrow hoofprint was unmistakable. It was the same print Nantaje had discovered back at Lionel's cabin.

The morning warmed under the late summer sun as the men worked at replacing the old boards in the corrals. They were working on a string of fencing that bent away from the stream and zigzagged along the uneven terrain back toward the barn when Blake suddenly looked over and watched Rachel leave the house and angle toward the barn. He straightened up and dragged a shirtsleeve across his forehead. "Whew, sure is getting hot," he announced.

The distant ringing of hammer against anvil drifted down from the blacksmith's shed located near the barn.

"Aye," O'Brian said, driving a nail through a fence board and giving it a final whack. He straightened up too, groaned and kneaded the muscles at the small of his back. "I think I'd rather be blowing up beaver dams. Least up in those hills the trees give some shade."

Blake's eyes followed the girl as she disappeared through a side door. Keane held back a grin. He reckoned she was tending her horse, and that Blake was itching to be with her. "We've been at this all morning," he said. "How about we all take a break?"

Blake unbuckled the nail pouch and dropped it and his hammer onto the wagon bed. "I'm for that."

"Half an hour," Keane called as Blake trotted off for his horse, tied a few dozen yards back down the fence line. He swung up onto its back and started toward the barn.

"He's in some kind of hurry," O'Brian noted.

"The kid has females on the brain."

"Hmm?"

"Rachel Jacob." Keane hitched a thumb toward the barn. "She just went in there."

"Oh," he said, understanding. "A young, healthy lass should keep the boy's attention for a while."

Keane settled his view on the blacksmith's shed. "Now might be a good time to have a look at those rifles. I've got some questions for Harvey. I'll go ask them, and that will give you a few uninterrupted minutes in the bunkhouse."

They gathered their horses and O'Brian rode to the bunkhouse while Keane went to pay a visit to the blacksmith. He found Harvey Oldebrook shaping a glowing horseshoe upon his anvil, his hammer blows ringing in the heat of the open furnace. The air inside the shed was humid, and sweat flowed freely down the farrier's grimy face. Just outside a horse was snubbed to a post. The animal eyed Keane warily as he stopped inside the wide, open doors.

Harvey looked up when Keane's shadow fell across his work. "Oh, hello there, John," he said, plunging the glowing shoe into a barrel of water and sending a cloud of steam toward the dark rafters overhead.

"Harvey."

The farrier wiped the shoe on a rag and bent for the horse's hind hoof to test the fit of the newly shaped and pierced shoe. "Figure by now the trial is well under way. What do you think?" Harvey went back to his anvil and gave the shoe a couple of taps, then grabbed a hammer, shoved a handful of nails into his mouth and levered the horse's leg up onto his knee.

"I wouldn't know."

Harvey laughed and mumbled something as he held the shoe in place and extracted a nail from his mouth. He hammered it through the hoof and quickly and expertly drove and set the rest of the nails, then released the leg. "I said, Judge Canaby gets things done in a timely fashion, if you know what I mean."

"I know. But is he a fair man?"

"Fair?" Harvey gave a short laugh. "I suppose that depends on which end of the rope you're on—the holding end or the wearing end. I can tell you this much: if I ever have to stand before him, I just hope it ain't for a hanging crime. There is a permanent gallows built out behind the jailhouse. That's because when Canaby was elected, it got too expensive rebuilding the thing every time we had a new hanging."

"Will Lionel get a fair hearing from Canaby?"

Harvey thought, then frowned and shook his head. "I'd like to believe so, but I'd be lying to you if I said I thought he would."

"Why is that?"

"For one thing, he's got two witnesses to go against him."

"And the other thing?" Keane asked when Harvey went silent.

Harvey hesitated, not sure how to proceed. "Let's just say that in this here country there are two kinds of justice. There's the white justice that's good for folks like you and me. And then there is the other kind, black justice. That's for folks like Lionel. I'm afraid a mixture of that black justice with a judge like Canaby sitting on the bench doesn't make it look too good for someone like Lionel.

"I like Lionel. He had his ways, and sometimes those ways grated on people. He liked to be alone. He lived away out there all by himself because he liked it that way. He always figured himself for something of an outcast. But he sure knew his horses. He was a good man with them horses, all right."

Harvey took a pair of tongs and grabbed out another shoe from a bed of coals, and the air filled once again with the ringing of his hammer. He expertly shaped and sized it, then thrust it back into the coals and pumped the bellows until sparks danced up through them, brightening them white-hot. Harvey glanced over from where he was working the big wooden lever and said, "Something you wanted to see me about?"

Keane pushed away from the wall and grabbed the lever. "I'll work the bellows a while."

"Thanks." Harvey took down another five or six rough-formed shoes off a peg and spaced them out through the coals.

"Actually, there was something." Keane had found a comfortable rhythm and the coals were sparking and glowing like the sun. "I noticed some tracks a while ago. Looks to me like you have a horse on this place with a narrow hoof. Figured you already knew about it, but if you didn't I just wanted you to know."

"That would be Casey's bay. Yep, I know about it. She was raised right here on the ranch, not one we took off the range. She got her hoof caught and wedged tight between some boulders when she was only a colt. Must have been stuck like that a day or two before we found her and pulled her free. The hoof healed up all right except it grew kinda narrow. But it don't bother her none. In fact, she's one of the sweetest fillies on the place. Real gentle and easygoing. Smart as a new penny, with natural-born cow sense about her. She's Casey's favorite and he don't let nobody ride her but himself. He keeps her in the barn, not with the others in the big corral."

"Seems I didn't need to bother you with it after all," Keane said.

Harvey plucked a glowing shoe from the coals and put it on the anvil, reaching for a piercing chisel. "I appreciate you keeping your eyes open for things like that, John. Next time you notice something wrong with one of these animals, you just let me know."

"I'll do that."

When Keane left the blacksmith he didn't see O'Brian anywhere around and figured the old Irishman must still be inside the bunkhouse checking the rifles. Keane started toward the pump beyond the barn, came around the corner of the building and stopped suddenly. Not a dozen feet ahead of him were Rachel and Blake. They were talking about something important by the worried expression on the girl's face. So riveted was their attention on each other that they didn't see him. He quickly backpedaled out of sight, but not before seeing Blake's back suddenly go ramrod straight and Rachel, on the verge of tears, all at once fling herself into his arms and bury her head into his shoulder. Blake tried awkwardly to comfort her. He was clearly upset too.

Keane figured he'd seen more than he should have, and he would have never purposefully spy on them.

But as he made his way along the other side of the barn to the water barrel by the hand pump and ladled out a cool drink for himself, he couldn't help but wonder what they had been talking about.

Chapter Eleven

O'Brian found Keane at the pump. He quenched his thirst, then told him that he'd not found a rifle that matched the one they were looking for in the bunkhouse.

" 'Course, some of the men took their guns with them," O'Brian concluded.

"Or maybe the gun we are looking for is in Casey's house." Keane told him what Harvey Oldebrook had said.

"Casey?" O'Brian thought this over and nodded his head. "That makes sense. After all, who would benefit most by Driscoll's death?"

As they went for their horses, Keane said, "Did you check Blake's rifle?"

"Nope. It weren't there."

"He had one when he rode in. I saw it on his horse."

"Then maybe it's still there," O'Brian said. "You don't think the kid did it, do you?"

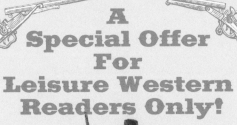

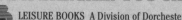

GET YOUR 4
FREE* BOOKS NOW—
A VALUE BETWEEN
$16 AND $20

Mail the Free* Book Certificate Today!

FREE* BOOKS
CERTIFICATE!

YES! I want to subscribe to the Leisure Western Book Club. Please send me my 4 FREE* BOOKS. Then, each month, I'll receive the four newest Leisure Western Selections to preview FREE* for 10 days. If I decide to keep them, I will pay the Special Member's Only discounted price of just $3.36 each, a total of $13.44 ($14.50 US in Canada). This saves me between $3 and $6 off the bookstore price. There are no shipping, handling or other charges.* There is no minimum number of books I must buy and I may cancel the program at any time. In any case, the 4 FREE* BOOKS are mine to keep—at a value of between $17 and $20!

*In Canada, add $5.00 Canadian shipping and handling per order for first shipment. For all subsequent shipments to Canada the cost of membership in the Book Club is $14.50 US, which includes $7.50 shipping and handling per month. All payments must be made in US currency.

Name _____

Address _____

City_____ State_____ Country_____

Zip_____ Telephone_____

If under 18, parent or guardian must sign. Terms, prices and conditions subject to change. Subscription subject to acceptance. Leisure Books reserves the right to reject any order or cancel any subscription.

Tear here and mail your FREE* book card today!

Get Four Books Totally
F R E E* –
A Value between
$16 and $20

Tear here and mail your FREE* book card today!

PLEASE RUSH
MY FOUR FREE*
BOOKS TO ME
RIGHT AWAY!

LeisureWestern Book Club
P.O. Box 6613
Edison, NJ 08818-6613

AFFIX
STAMP
HERE

"I don't know. From what I've heard so far of Egan Driscoll, and the men who worked for him, any one of them would have been pleased to see him dead."

They rode back to where they had left off on the corrals and resumed their work of replacing the damaged boards. A few minutes later Blake showed up. Concern smoldered in his eyes, and a frown cut deep into his face. He stepped down off his horse and tied it to a post. Without saying a word he buckled the nail pouch about his narrow waist, took up his hammer and began driving nails into the fence.

"You look like someone just stomped all over your favorite hat," O'Brian said.

Blake glanced up. "It's nothing."

"If it's nothing, then how come you just nailed that old board we just pulled off back in place?" O'Brian asked.

"I did?" Blake stared at the splintered plank of wood he had pounded to the post.

Keane grinned. "Forget it. It's plain you are worried about something. Couldn't help but see you and Rachel talking. Something happen between you two?"

"No," he said too quickly. "That is, not between Rachel and me," he went on, looking worried. Then he gave a short, uncertain laugh. "She just told me that her mother wants to take her away with her. Back east to St. Louis. To stay with her aunt."

"For a visit?"

Blake looked over. "Forever."

"Oh." Keane remembered the remark he had heard the afternoon he and O'Brian arrived at the Lazy J. "Then it is true, about Mrs. Jacob and Driscoll."

"You know?"

"Word gets around," Keane said.

Blake stared at the ground. "It's true. Rachel said her

Pa confronted Felicity about it the day after Driscoll was killed." Blake's fist tightened into a hard knot about the hammer and he suddenly flung it against a fence board. "That man's death has wormed its way into all of our lives. Now Felicity is leaving John, and she's taking Rachel with her."

"Rachel's old enough to make up her own mind," Keane said.

"Maybe. But is she strong enough to stand up to her mother?"

O'Brian said, "Ya mean to tell me that John Jacob knew his wife was playing him for a cuckold?"

"I don't know how long he knew it. But he knew."

O'Brian caught Keane's eye. Keane read what he was thinking. The same thought had occurred to him just then too.

"Do you know where John Jacob was the evening Driscoll was murdered?" Keane asked.

Blake shrugged. "No. I'd left the ranch by that time." All at once he looked up. "I know what you're driving at, but get it out of your head. Mr. Jacob ain't a murderer—I mean, not that Driscoll didn't get what he had coming, the way he treated folks. But Mr. Jacob didn't kill him. It was Lionel. We all know that. Everybody knows that Lionel shot him." Blake's eyes narrowed. "But *you* don't believe that, do you? *You* think that Lionel might be innocent." Sudden concern rose in Blake's voice, and the young man tried to hide it.

Keane said, "The way I heard it, nobody actually saw Lionel shoot Driscoll. The two men with him were down by the corral when it happened. They heard a shot, and that was all."

"You're getting mighty nosy about something that don't concern you."

"It's a man's duty to get nosy if an innocent life is at

stake," Keane said. "If Lionel did kill Driscoll, then he deserves to swing for it, no matter how much the man was hated. But if he didn't, a murderer goes free, and what's to stop him from killing again?"

"It ain't going to happen again," Blake said confidently, then added quickly, "once they put a rope around his neck." Blake pulled a board off the back of the wagon and hauled it down the line to the next section.

O'Brian said softly, "The kid is mighty touchy all of a sudden, ain't he? Almost like he's hiding something."

They moved the wagon down to where Blake was working and off-loaded enough boards to repair another dozen sections of old fencing. No more was said about Lionel, or Rachel's leaving for St. Louis, but Blake's mood had gone sour, and there was little talk about anything other than the job they were doing.

They used up the last few nails at the bottom of the keg and Blake said he knew where they were stored and that he'd go get a new keg from the storage shed.

"A nail keg this size must weigh eighty pounds. Need some help with it?" Keane offered, tugging leather work gloves off his fingers.

"I can manage all right. You two take it easy." There was a condescending note in Blake's voice. Keane took it to mean that since he and O'Brian were old enough to be his father and grandfather, they needed the rest.

Keane grinned. "All right. Us old codgers will catch our breath under that tree over there until you get back."

Blake cracked a smile at that. "I didn't mean it to sound that way, really."

O'Brian laughed. "I don't know about John here, but this codger can sure do with a break."

Blake climbed aboard the wagon, flicked the reins

and got the team moving. The rig rolled off in the direction of the barn but veered to the left of it instead and swung around a corner.

They started for the tree, and the spot of shade it offered. But just then a screen door slammed. Rachel rushed out of the house, into the yard and wheeled back to face her mother, who was right on her heels. Keane and O'Brian were not so far from the house that they couldn't hear Rachel's words, and the anger in her voice.

"It's not fair. I'm not going with you, and you can't make me!"

Felicity Jacob marched up to her defiant daughter and said, "You will go." She took Rachel by the shoulders. "Don't you think I know what's best?" Felicity noted Keane and O'Brian standing there. "Let's go back into the house."

Rachel was in tears and she twisted free of her mother's grasp. "No. I'm not going in there with you."

Felicity tried to calm her, but Rachel pulled away and fled toward the barn, clumsily gathering up her skirt to keep from tripping in her headlong flight. Felicity cast a worried look at the two men, then back at Rachel, as the girl flung open a side door and rushed inside.

"What was that all about?" O'Brian wondered.

"Imagine it has something to do with her ma wanting to take her back east."

"The gal just might have the gumption to go again' her ma."

"Maybe," Keane allowed.

Felicity stood there, as if uncertain whether to go after her daughter or let the girl blow off steam on her own. She had just started back for the house. Suddenly the barn door opened and a horse leaped from it with the girl on its back. Riding bareback with her skirts bunched up around her and the pink skin of her exposed legs flashing in the sunlight as they clutched at the horse's flanks, Rachel leaned low into the wind. She aimed the animal toward the hills and let it carry her away from the house, running at a reckless gallop over the uneven ground.

"That gal is gonna break her fool neck," O'Brian declared.

Felicity's mouth fell open and her eyes stretched wide. Keane shifted his view back to the fleeing girl, receding toward the higher land that rimmed the ranch like a bowl. She was riding as if she *wanted* to break her neck. Keane shook his head and untied his horse from the fence.

"I better go after her."

"Think chasing her down is a smart thing to do?" O'Brian wondered.

"Riding like that, the kid is liable to run right over a cliff and never know it."

Keane swung up onto his horse and kicked it into motion. He managed to keep Rachel in sight until the land rose and the forested hillside finally hid her from his view. But her trail was not hard to follow, not the sort of thing Nantaje might puzzle over, as he had Ridere's trace a few days before. Rachel's racing horse left deep tracks that were easy to follow.

He did not gain on her right away. Common sense kept Keane from letting his horse run full out, and he held the animal to a safe gallop, all the while knowing that the distance was widening.

As he rode, he had to wonder if it wasn't an emotional outburst like this that had injured her own horse. He only hoped Rachel was expert enough a horsewoman to remain with the animal, and that the animal didn't stumble and throw her.

But almost as that thought came to him, he came over a low rise and spied the shape upon the ground. It wasn't moving. A few dozen feet away her horse lay upon its side, thrashing the air with its hooves.

"Damn," he cursed aloud. Scrambling down a rocky slope, Keane reined to a halt and leaped to the ground. As he went to Rachel, her downed horse squealed in pain nearby. Keane knelt at Rachel's side and carefully turned her over.

Her eyes opened and she groaned softly. With a shaking hand, she ran fingers up into her hair and touched a swelling lump and grimaced.

"Looks like a bad bump on your head there," Keane said.

"My ankle," she said.

He felt it through the leather of her shoes. "It doesn't feel broken."

"Hurts." Rachel was groggy.

He looked into her eyes, relieved to see the pupils responding quickly. "Do you hurt anywhere else?"

"I . . . I don't think so."

"Need to get you home. Can you stand?"

She attempted to lever herself up. He gave her a hand off the ground. "The horse? Please see how he is," she said, more concerned about the animal than herself.

Keane glanced over at the animal, then helped her a few paces to a tree and sat her gently against it. "Wait here."

Its leg was broken. It was a bad break, with the bone poking through the flesh and a pool of blood soaking the dirt. Keane grimaced and knew there was only one remedy for a break like that. He stood and went back to his horse for his rifle.

"Do you have to?" Rachel asked, her voice strained, her eyes wide.

"It's real bad, Miss Jacob, and it looks like an artery was cut too."

Rachel understood. She didn't say any more and turned her eyes away. She flinched when the rifle boomed. Keane came back, grim-faced, and helped her to his horse, sweeping her up into his big arms as if she weighed no more than a kitten and placing her lightly onto his saddle. He mounted behind her and started back to the ranch.

"He was one of Papa's favorites," she said softly after a moment.

"Reckon you will have some explaining to do."

"Yes, I will."

"Least we can be grateful you only suffered a knock on the head and a twisted ankle."

"I deserved more," she replied sadly.

"Now, don't get too down on yourself. You aren't the first daughter to go crossways with a mother."

"You saw?"

"You two weren't exactly trying very hard to keep it among yourselves."

"You heard too?"

He detected the alarm in her voice and gave a short laugh. "Not much. But enough to know you were mighty upset. That's why I came after you. I figured you might get yourself in trouble riding off like a wild Apache."

She looked back at him. "That's the second time you have mentioned them, Mr. Keane."

"Mentioned who?"

"Apache."

"Is it?"

"Yes. The first time was when you came up behind me in the yard."

He looked past her and saw the ranch come into view far out in the valley. They had come farther than he had realized. "Well, maybe that is because I've spent so much time among them."

"Really? You lived with the Apache?"

"Lived with a few. But mostly I fought them."

"When?"

"When I was in the army. I was a major under General Crook's command. I retired a few years back."

"You are not old. Why did you retire?"

Keane grimaced, but she didn't see it. "There was a colonel who had certain ideas on how the Apache should be handled. I didn't happen to agree with him on most things. One day he gave the orders for my company to pursue a band of fleeing Chiricahua down into a canyon of the Salt River. They were mostly women and children, about forty people in all. Might have been all of four warriors among them, yet we were ordered to pursue. This particular colonel made it clear he wasn't interested in taking prisoners, and I had to make a choice."

"What did you do?"

"When we came on them, I ordered my troops not to attack. There was an overly eager young lieutenant who took particular offense at not being allowed to kill a few dozen helpless Apache. He filed a report, and that report reached the desk of General Crook."

"That wasn't good, was it?"

"No, ma'am. That was not good. Even though General Crook agreed with me in principle, there was the little matter of discipline, and disobeying an order. Only the army didn't consider it little. It would be wrong to overlook it, even though the order was a bad one. I was facing a military court. Crook gave me the choice of retiring, or the court-martial."

"You sound bitter."

Keane *was* bitter. Although he had tried to put the past behind him, he'd not gotten over the disgrace of being forced from the service. "I made the decision to disobey that order. No one else did it. Now I have to live with it. That is just the way life is, Miss Jacob. A person reaps the fruits of what he sows. Men and women have to stand up and take responsibility for their actions, or they are not much of men or women. It would have been cowardly, and I would have brought dishonor to myself, if I had done otherwise. No, Miss Jacob, I have no one to blame but myself, and it would have been wrong for me to try."

She was silent a few seconds; then she said softly, "Is that what you meant last night when you said some people did things out of honor or disgrace?"

Her question stung him. Maybe she even felt his muscles tighten slightly where she leaned back against him. "Yes, ma'am. You've got an eye for reading people's feelings."

"Sorry." Rachel was quiet after that, as if thinking over what he had told her. At the house Keane slid off the horse, lifted Rachel down and carried her inside.

Felicity took one look at her daughter in his arms and gasped, "Oh my God! Is she hurt?"

"A knock on the head and a twisted ankle is all, I think."

"Bring her up here." She hurried up the stairs ahead of them, opened the door to Rachel's bedroom and stepped aside as Keane carried the girl into the room and set her in a chair.

Felicity began unbuttoning the shoe. "Riding off like

that was a reckless thing to do. You could have been killed," she scolded, quickly popping buttons through their loops.

"I'm sorry," Rachel said.

Felicity slipped off the shoe and began rolling down the girl's stocking.

"I'll just let myself out," Keane said.

"Thank you for going after her and bringing her home."

He nodded.

Rachel said, "Papa's horse broke a leg. Mr. Keane had to put it down."

Felicity frowned briefly. "Thank you for taking care of that too."

Keane closed the door behind him and went down the stairs. He had started across the parlor when he suddenly changed his mind. Glancing up the staircase and seeing that he was momentarily alone, he crossed to John Jacob's office and went inside.

It was as he remembered the place; the only sound there at that moment was the large clock ticking softly in the corner. Keane crossed to the rifle rack and removed Jacob's Winchester from the wall rack and levered open the breech.

"What are you doing in here?"

Keane stiffened and turned. Blake was standing in the doorway, staring hard at him. Keane grinned easily and hefted the Winchester casually. "I was just looking at Mr. Jacob's rifle here."

"Why? It's just an ordinary rifle." Blake looked around the office, then out into the hallway.

Keane wondered what kind of reaction the truth might get from the kid. He figured he'd see. "I was just wondering if this might not be the rifle that killed Egan Driscoll."

Scowling, Blake strode across the office and took the rifle from him. "What kind of crazy notion is that? We all know who killed Driscoll." He put it back in the rack. "I don't think Mr. Jacob would much appreciate being accused of murder, nor you looking though his things."

"Wonder why everyone is so dead set on seeing Lionel swing at the end of a rope."

"Maybe you better leave now."

"Maybe I better." Keane started toward the door.

Blake said, "I saw you carry Rachel in here. Was she hurt?"

"Her horse threw her. She's upstairs with her ma right now."

Keane felt Blake's eyes burning into his back all the way across the parlor and out the front door.

Chapter Twelve

O'Brian was waiting for Keane on the front porch when he came out. "What happened to the girl?"

"You called it, Dougal. She nearly broke her neck. Horse broke its leg. I took care of that."

"When Blake saw you ride up with Rachel he hauled himself back to the house faster than shucked corn down a hungry chicken."

"She should be all right." Keane led his horse toward the barn. Harvey Oldebrook intercepted them and asked what had happened.

"Rachel's always been an impulsive gal." Oldebrook shook his head and followed it with a brief laugh. "You wouldn't expect such a gentle gal like that could flare up like she does. Takes after her pa in that respect. You hardly ever see Mr. Jacob lose his temper, but when he does, you best just stand clear of him. Too bad about the mare. Mr. Jacob's gonna be right put out to hear about it." Harvey went back to his shop.

Keane tied his horse to the hitching post and peered at the wagon sitting in the distance by the corral. Then he narrowed his eyes at the sky and said, "Let's bring in those horses and call it a day, Dougal."

They turned the horses into the corral and put the hammers and saws in the tool shed. When they finished Keane swung up onto his horse.

"Where you headed to now?" O'Brian asked.

"It's about time someone tries to talk sense into Harry. Want to ride along?"

O'Brian considered a moment and shook his head. "I think I'll just hang around here the rest of the day. Still got half a bottle of tequila in my saddlebag, and she's been calling my name ever since we arrived here."

"You take care Casey don't find you drunk when he and the other's get back from town."

"I'll keep the boss in mind. Say, wonder how the trial's gone?"

Keane frowned. "I don't know, but if I was a betting man, my money would be with the hangman. Lionel was as good as hanged the moment they closed the bars on him. Everyone believed it so, and no one seems much interested in hearing any other story."

"I find that kind of strange, don't you, John?"

"There is a lot about all this I find strange."

"Too bad we couldn't have found something to save the poor man's hide."

"Too bad. I reckon now his neck depends on someone coming forward."

"You mean like Harry?"

Keane nodded. "After all, Harry is the only eyewitness there is."

"Would anyone believe him now?"

"They'd at least have to listen to what he had to say."

O'Brian grimaced. "Maybe you *better* try and talk some sense into Harry."

"I intend to." Keane turned his horse from the hitching rail and started away from the ranch.

When the door opened Harrison Ridere was leaning on the crutch, looking fitter than Keane last remembered him.

"You must be feeling better, Harry."

"Nantaje been taking good care of this child. Get down off that horse and come on inside. Got hot coffee and a couple baking sage hens."

Keane turned his reins about a post and followed Ridere inside. He was alone. Keane asked about the others.

"Nantaje is off hunting. He spends most of his time out there somewhere, and when he does come back, he always has fresh game with him. Haven't eaten this good since the day I walked away from Fort Huachuca. As far as Louvel goes, I haven't heard a word from him since he left a couple of days ago." Ridere's easy way became suddenly sober. "What do you hear about Lionel?"

Keane tossed his hat onto the back of a chair and sat on the edge of the rumpled bed. "Trial was today. Nearly every man on the Lazy J went to it. I haven't heard how he fared, but since everyone already figured him for guilty, my guess is, the trial was just a formality to make the hanging legal."

They heard a horse approach the cabin. Royden Louvel came through the door, brushing the trail dust from his clothes with his left hand, the empty sleeve of his right arm pinned up at his side.

"This country is so damned dry, a man might choke to death on the dust of it."

Keane ladled out a drink of water for him from a bucket. Louvel swilled the water in his mouth and spat it out the door, then drank deeply to slack his thirst.

"You've been in Mariposa Springs all this time?" Keane asked.

"Ah have."

"More than likely behind a card table," Ridere quipped.

"Ah have done some of that too," Louvel freely admitted, "but mostly Ah have been keeping an eye on what was going on with that Negro friend of yours, Harry."

"And what has been going on?" Harry asked worriedly.

"There was a trial today, and it was a joke if Ah ever seen one. They found a defense attorney for Lionel who had no more interest in defending him than he did in sticking his own neck in the noose. Then there were those two eyewitnesses."

"Johnson and Lomis," Keane said.

"Yes, Ah believe those are their names. It was clear they had not seen the murder, only heard the shot. There was no one to defend Lionel." Louvel looked at Ridere. "The only real witness to the murder was here, hiding from the sheriff because of his indiscretions."

Ridere looked away from Louvel's accusing eyes and stared at the floor.

"They found him guilty?" Keane asked, even though the answer was clear.

"Yes."

"The sentence?"

"The usual requirement for the taking of another man's life. Hanging."

"When?"

"Tomorrow," Louvel said. "Eleven o'clock. There is a gallows already standing behind the jailhouse. It appears hangings are a regular event in Mariposa Springs. It is not a town in which Ah wish to get caught breaking the law."

Ridere's head snapped up. "Tomorrow! So soon?"

"Apparently the judge is a man who believes in swift justice."

"Except this isn't justice!"

Keane said, "Then maybe the time has come for you to put the record straight."

Ridere dreaded facing Sheriff Hodgeback, a man whose wife he had taken and pleasured. Sure, she had practically demanded it of him, but there was no denying a husband's right to vengeance when such a thing happens, and when that husband happens to be a gun-toting lawman . . . well, the prospects for Ridere looked bleak. No one would fault Walter Hodgeback for demanding his pound of flesh—and taking it.

But Lionel's prospects for seeing another sunset after today were pretty bleak too. Lionel had practically saved his life, and unlike Ridere, who was guilty, Lionel was innocent.

"I'll go. I'll tell them what I saw," Ridere said. Using the crutch, he hobbled to the door and stood there. The sun was low in the west, and not much daylight remained. "I'll go first thing in the morning." He turned back and sat wearily at the table, glancing at Louvel and Keane. "Will you two ride with me?"

"I need to get back to the Lazy J and tell O'Brian, but I'll be in town tomorrow for the hanging. And I'm sure most of the ranch hands will be there too," Keane said.

"Ah will ride with you," Louvel said.

"Where are you two going?" A shadow had darkened the doorway. Nantaje was standing there, the hind quarter of an antelope slung over his shoulder.

Ridere said, "Lionel was found guilty. I gotta go into

town and tell what I saw before they put the noose around his neck."

"When is the hanging?"

"Tomorrow," Keane and Louvel said together.

The Apache's face remained expressionless. Whatever he was thinking, he wasn't showing it. He dropped the fresh meat on the table in front of Ridere and with his sharp scalping knife, began to remove the hide. After a moment Nantaje said, "It should have never gotten as far as a trial, Harry."

Ridere frowned. "I know." It was plain from the way Keane and Louvel looked at him that they were thinking the same thing.

"All right. So I've been a coward. I should have gone into town as soon as I was able to ride and told what I saw. I should have taken my licks from that sheriff. I didn't. I was wrong. All right? You all satisfied?"

Keane stood off the edge of the bed and took his hat from the chair back. "I'll see you in town tomorrow. Don't be late."

"You want to stay and eat?" Nantaje asked as he butchered the meat he had brought in.

"No thanks. I need to get back. The men should be back from town by now. Want to hear what they have to say." Keane tugged his hat onto his head and stepped outside. Evening shadows had lengthened across the ground. The cottonwood trees just below the cabin where the ambusher had fired from were already in deep shade. He stepped up into his saddle and saw Louvel leaning in the doorway, watching him.

"What have you learned there at the ranch?" the gambler asked in his soft, southern voice.

"A few things. For one, Egan Driscoll was hated by just about everyone who knew him. For two, whoever pulled the trigger came from the Lazy J. And for three, there are at least four people with good reasons for wanting to see him dead."

A thin smile moved across Royden Louvel's weathered face. "And on which of these four have you put your money, suh?"

Keane laughed. "Spoken like a true gambler."

With a flourish, Louvel swept off his hat and bowed deeply from the waist like an actor receiving accolades at the end of a performance.

"I think I'll just hold my cards close to my vest until I see how the game finally plays itself out."

Louvel straightened up, grinning. "You do that, but remember, this is not a game that Harry's friend can afford to lose."

"I'll keep that in mind, Mr. Louvel."

Keane left the lean, one-armed man standing there and started back to the Lazy J. He had hoped to reach the ranch before nightfall, but that seemed unlikely now with his shadow stretching far out in front of him. It was a rugged land; beautiful always, but sometimes lonely, like now. It was an unsettled country, shifting its moods with the ever-changing light of the day. A morning sun might pick out the sharp clef of a rocky ledge that a noon sun would miss, or that the muted evening light would soften with hues of grays and browns. It was a land that matched Keane's own restless spirit. The sort of place he could grow to love.

The trail passed through a cut between towering cliffs where shadows gathered quickly. Keane shivered as a cold finger of warning dragged up his spine. He was suddenly wary, his eyes in constant motion. His view climbed the dark, rocky walls that soared on either side of him, no more than a hundred yards apart. But he saw nothing threatening.

Keane had almost emerged on the other side of the pass when the shot boomed from the cliffs above and a spray of sandstone erupted just ahead of his horse. He bolted from the saddle and scrambled for the cover of the boulders alongside the trail as his horse galloped beyond the rocky walls and disappeared.

Two more shots rang out. A bullet ricocheted above his head, and the other took a gouge from an outcropping a few feet to his left. The shots came from across the way, halfway up the cliffs. Keane pegged the place at once by the muzzle flashes, but whoever was up there was staying out of sight. Instantly old instincts and years of training took over. He snapped off two quick shots in return, hardly aware of the report of his revolver as the weapon bucked in his fist. Across the way his bullets made small puffs of rock dust, and that was all. The bushwhacker was well concealed behind the rocks and impossible to hit from Keane's vantage point. But then, it would be the same for the man up there. A standoff. A game of nerves and patience. Keane had played such hands before, and he'd won against some of the finest guerrilla warriors ever born on this earth—the Apache.

But there was something different this time, and Keane had a feeling he'd not have a long wait. The rifle boomed again, then went silent. Keane remained behind the boulder another five minutes, then lifted his hat on a stick and held it in view long enough to know his ambusher had gone. The shadows had deepened. Keane lunged from cover, diving and rolling behind a stand of stunted scrub oak. As he suspected, no further shots stabbed from out of the darkness up there. Keane sprinted across the trail and flattened against the rocks, his Colt ready, although that small voice at the back of his head was declaring the battle was over.

He holstered his revolver and climbed to a ledge of rock and worked his way up to where the shots had come from. It was too dark to see much now, but it wasn't difficult to find three cartridges laying there. Keane shoved them into a pocket and worked his way along a narrow trail to the top of the pass. Nantaje might have followed it farther, but Keane's eyes lost it on the stony ground. There was nothing more there. Whoever had bushwhacked him had gone. But he would not be far off, Keane noted grimly as he turned one of the cartridges toward the last fading rays of light.

It had been fired from the same rifle that had killed Egan Driscoll.

He spent the next twenty minutes running down his horse, and when he got back to the bunkhouse the men of the Lazy J were all gathered around the long table. The mood was dark, the talk mainly about Lionel and the trial. Casey was with them, and so was John Jacob. Hardly anyone took notice of Keane when he came in. O'Brian had been drinking, and he grinned crookedly at him. It was plain that most of the other hands had been drinking too.

Keane sat on his bunk, eyeing the men; one of them was the bushwhacker. Dougal O'Brian came over and sat beside him. His eyes shifted around the room, and when he spoke it was in a whisper.

"Managed to check out Casey's place while you were gone. No rifle. When they came back from town, he had it with him. The jury found Lionel guilty. Gonna string him up in the morning. The men are pretty down about that."

"I heard. Louvel brought word of it while I was at the cabin."

"Did you convince Harry?"

"I didn't have to. Harry convinced himself. He's going into town in the morning before the hanging and tell Hodgeback what he saw."

"I know Harry, and I know that's a hard thing for him to do."

"It's hard, but it's the right thing to do and he knows it. Louvel and Nantaje are going to ride with him so he won't have to face the sheriff alone."

"I only hope the sheriff believes him. We haven't had much luck ferreting out the murderer here on our own."

"Not yet," Keane replied, certain the murderer was in this room right now. He glanced up to discover Blake standing not five feet away, holding a glass of whiskey and staring at them as if they had just risen from a long sleep out of a cold grave. Keane and Blake's eyes connected and Blake's jaw went rigid as he turned away.

"How much did he hear?" O'Brian wondered.

"I don't know." Did it even matter now? Maybe the time had come to announce their purpose there. If nothing else, it would save Lionel's neck from a stretching. But doing so would drive the real murderer deeper under cover, and Keane wanted to have someone to give to the sheriff in exchange for Lionel.

"Has Blake been here all the time?"

O'Brian shrugged, bleary-eyed from the liquor. "Far as I know he has." The Irishman paused to search his brain. He appeared to be having some difficulty in that endeavor. "Maybe he come in a little after. Yeah, that's right. He did came in later. I seen him through the window talking with Rachel out there behind the house where that gal feeds all them critters. Yep, they spent a while talking, then he come in sometime after dark . . . I think. Wasn't paying too much attention to Blake, what with all the talk going on about the trial." O'Brian considered a moment and said, "Why do you ask?"

"Someone bushwhacked me along the trail." No one was watching them and Keane stuck a hand into his pocket and gave O'Brian the three spent cartridges he'd found.

O'Brian peered at them. "They're from the same gun that killed Driscoll."

"That's right," Keane replied quietly. "Same gun, but not the same shooter."

"What do you mean?"

"Whoever killed Driscoll was a crack shot, but the person who bushwhacked me wasn't . . . or maybe he were just trying to miss. It was dusk, about the same time Driscoll was killed, and the distance no farther. But all the shots were wide."

"Sounds like he was trying to scare you off," O'Brian said.

"That's the way I see it. Someone knows what we are up to. Makes me think we're getting close to something, and that is making someone mighty nervous."

"And you think that someone might be Blake?"

Keane pulled thoughtfully at his chin, feeling the whiskers that had grown there the last few days. "Might be. Blake walked in on me while I was checking John Jacob's Winchester."

"Jacob?" O'Brian said, as if suddenly recalling something. He glanced at the long table where the owner of the Lazy J was sitting with some of the other men. "Come to think of it, Mr. Jacob didn't come to the bunkhouse right away either."

"And how about Casey? Did he come in with the others?"

O'Brian tried to remember but couldn't.

"It doesn't matter, I suppose," Keane said, and his attention shifted back to the table, where the talk had become louder. John Jacob's low voice carried in the noisy bunkhouse as he remarked on the trial.

"I respected the man. He knew his job and did it well. But in spite of that, it was plain he done the killing, and the jury passed fair judgment on him."

"Maybe," Weatherby replied dryly, lightly rapping an empty whiskey glass on the tabletop, "but no man here can claim Driscoll never did nothing to provoke it. Every man here—well, everyone but Lomis maybe— has had call to hate that man. But it was Lionel who had the guts to do something about it."

The men's voices rose in agreement. Keane smelled coffee brewing. Garwood was at the stove feeding wood into the firebox. Keane went for a cup of it. He needed coffee more than the whiskey the men were freely passing around.

"After tomorrow we can put all this behind us and life will get back to the way things were before," Jacob was saying confidently. "I'm personally gonna be relieved once it's all past."

Keane looked for Blake, but the kid had gone off somewhere. He moved to the window. In the darkness beyond only a couple of lights burning in the house across the way were visible. The kid had disappeared.

The men drifted off to their bunks as the hour grew late. Finally John Jacob told the men to be ready to ride early if they wanted to witness the hanging. He and Casey left together. Casey veered off toward his little house, while Jacob started across the dark yard toward the big stone house.

Keane lingered by the window, watching Jacob. Beneath the dark Mulberry trees something moved. A man stepped from the shadows. Although Keane could not see the face, he knew by the way he walked and stood that it was Blake.

The two men talked a moment, then suddenly they hurried across the dark yard toward the barn. A couple minutes later, Blake led a horse from it. He and Jacob stood there talking a while longer, then Blake swung up into his saddle and rode off into the night. Jacob stared into the darkness long after Blake had gone. Then, as if shaking himself from some weighty thought, he walked toward the house and went inside.

Keane was aware that someone had come up behind him. "What is it?" O'Brian asked, seeing his concern.

There were too many ears nearby for Keane to talk about it right there. "Nothing. Just looking out at the night." That satisfied O'Brian, and he staggered to his bunk.

But Keane was worried, although he could not know then exactly what it was that had raised the hairs on his neck.

Chapter Thirteen

As if the heavens themselves were protesting the coming injustice scheduled later that day, the skies were heavy with clouds. There was a cool wind moving slowly through the little valley where the Lazy J nestled between the hills.

A few miles away Harrison Ridere was peering through the dingy window at the gloomy sky, holding a cup of coffee. "Not looking forward to this day," he said, frowning.

"Looks like we might be getting some rain," Louvel commented.

Nantaje studied the angry clouds and said, "Maybe later." The Apache went outside to bring their horses up from the corral.

Louvel looked at Ridere and, seeing his long face, he gave a laugh. "Don't worry about it. If the sheriff shoots first and asks questions later, Ah'll see to it you get a decent burial."

"Not funny, Louvel." Ridere limped back to the bed and sat down. The leg still pained him, but the swelling had gone down some, and Nantaje had predicted a complete recovery. He sucked in a short, quick breath and said, "I just want to get this over with."

"Nantaje and I will be right behind you all the way."

Ridere frowned and stood again, resting his weight on the crutch. They heard the horses come up.

"That was quick," Louvel noted, reaching for his hat.

"Nantaje is not wasting any time, is he?" Ridere said gloomily.

Louvel reached for the door, but as his hand touched the latch it suddenly burst open and three men crowded inside, guns drawn. Louvel's hand stabbed for the Spiller and Burr revolver at his side.

One of the men swung out. A gun slammed hard into the side of Louvel's head. The one-armed man staggered back and crumpled to the floor among a small avalanche of pots and pans from the shelf on the wall there.

Ridere swung up his crutch and grabbed it in both hands, Commanche war lance fashion. But the Colt .45 that leveled between his eyes and glared back at him from its big bore froze Ridere in his tracks.

"Go ahead and try it," the man behind the trigger growled, "and I'll plow a hole through your skull wide enough to drive a mule train through."

Ridere dropped the crutch.

Louvel groaned and tried to push himself up off the floor. The third man came all the way inside the cabin and snatched Louvel's revolver out of his holster. "That was a dumb move, mister." He helped Louvel into a chair and stepped back out of reach.

Ridere said, "Who are you? What's going on here?"

"I'm Clint Cadell, foreman of the Bar Sixteen ranch.

Our land borders the Lazy J just yonder of the rise past this cabin, over there. And you're trespassing on Lazy J land."

"We're here with the owner's permission," Ridere shot back.

"Is that the story you're telling?"

Holding a hand to his head, Louvel said, "It's the truth. John Jacob said we could stay here until Harry is fit to travel."

Cadell huffed through his nose as if that was just about the most ridiculous thing he'd ever heard.

"Go ask him yourself right now," Ridere challenged.

"I couldn't do that even if I wanted to 'cause, you see, right about now Mr. Jacob is heading into Mariposa Springs to watch a hanging. But it was a nice try anyway, and I might even have bitten on that hook. But if what you say is true, why would John Jacob have sent a telegram to the Bar Sixteen last night asking if we'd check up on this place for him, since him and his men were gonna be to the hanging today? Seems some of his hands have reported smoke coming from this cabin, and since Jacob's bronc buster is high and dry in Hodgeback's jail, that can only mean someone has moved in. Jacob said he has lost some cows of late and was suspecting some brand artists might be working ahead of the roundup. Mr. Jacob sent us out here to hold whoever we found here for him until he gets back."

"That can't be true," Louvel said. "And even if it was, there was no call to burst in on us like we were common outlaws."

"No?" Cadell took Louvel's gun from his partner and showed it to him. "Don't tell me you wouldn't have used this if I'd given you a chance to draw it."

"Only to protect myself from strangers with guns of

their own, suh." Louvel came back, his head clearing rapidly now, his wits returning.

"Mr. Jacob warned us that whoever was up here might try something like that." Cadell glanced around the place and said, "You two alone here?"

Ridere started to speak, but Louvel cut him off. "It is just the two of us, suh."

Cadell looked suspiciously at Ridere, then at Louvel. He didn't believe him. "Larry, go take a look around the place. Check out that barn. I get the feeling these two are stringing us a line."

"Right, boss."

Louvel caught a glimpse of the man through the window, heading down to the barn, where Nantaje had gone a few minutes earlier. He didn't understand what had happened, what had changed Jacob's mind. But he did know that they were wasting valuable time while every minute spent here brought Lionel another minute closer to his execution. Ridere needed to get into town soon or Lionel was going to swing for another man's crime.

Louvel said, "Take us into Mariposa Springs now. Let us face Jacob in person."

"I see no reason to make that ride, mister. Jacob said to hold you here until he gets back, and that's just what I intend to do."

"That man they are hanging is innocent. Harry saw it all. He can prove it. But we have to get to town to do so."

"You are a slick talker too, mister, like your friend here. But I'm not about to believe anything you have to tell me. Now, just settle down and don't cause me no trouble unless you want me to tie you to that chair."

The other man there pulled a chair around and

straddled it, resting his gun hand across its back. Cadell stepped to the door and cast a look down toward the barns, then put his attention back on Ridere and Louvel.

Louvel considered the guns covering them and knew that if they were going to get into town in time to save Lionel, it was going to have to be up to Nantaje now.

Cadell glanced out the door again and then back with an impatient scowl upon his sunburned face. "Soon as Larry gets back we'll lock these hombres in this cabin. It will be a whole lot easier watching them that way than trying to keep them covered until Jacob comes for them."

Louvel palmed the deck of cards laying on the table and began shuffling them one-handed. Cadell kept one eye out the door, but like his partner he was intrigued, watching this one-armed man's fingers manipulate the deck, cutting it, shuffling cards, then putting the deck back together.

"Hey, that's a pretty clever trick," the man straddling the chair said.

"It is really not hard once you train your fingers. The movement is most unnatural at first," Louvel told him, neatly dealing out two piles of cards, then setting the deck down and taking up his hand.

The man picked up his and studied them.

"Care to place a bet?" Louvel asked.

"I ain't got no money on me," he answered with half a grin.

"Put those cards down, Frank," Cadell said. "Don't you see he's trying to distract you?"

It appeared to Louvel that Frank would have welcomed the distraction, but the man dropped the cards on the table anyway and stood.

"Wonder what's keeping Larry?" Cadell mumbled.

Frank went outside and shaded his eyes toward the barn. "Want me to go see what he's up to?"

"No . . . not yet. Give him a couple more minutes."

"Maybe he found himself a woman back there," Frank quipped.

Cadell grinned. "That would be just like him, wouldn't it?"

"Hey, recollect last spring in Durango?"

Cadell's grin widened and he nodded at the memory. "I remember. It would be just Larry's luck to find himself a good-looking lady way out here miles from town." Then his smile faded as his concern returned. "But that ain't likely to happen today."

Cadell's view shifted from Ridere to Louvel. "Who's down there?"

"Ah already told you. No one is down there."

"And I told you, you're stringing us a line, mister." Cadell looked at Frank. "Go see what's happened to Larry. And keep your eyes peeled."

"Don't worry about me," Frank said confidently.

"Maybe there's a wild Indian down there," Louvel suggested when Cadell stepped back inside.

Cadell just shot him a narrow look and shook his head. "Why, you must be dumber than dirt, mister. There ain't no wild Injuns in these parts."

Louvel only shrugged and permitted a faint smile to touch his lips. "Ah'm from out of town."

"You can say that again."

"How many?"

"Tw—two more," Larry croaked. It was difficult to talk with his head yanked full back by the hair and the glinting edge of a scalping knife poised half an inch above his throat.

142

"Why have you come?" Nantaje demanded, his voice as sharp as the knife in his fist, but subdued so as not to carry beyond the walls of the horse stall where he had pinned Larry to the ground and was keeping him with a knee jammed hard against his spine.

"We were told there might be rustlers holed up here."

"Who told you that?"

"Mr. Jacob."

"You work for him?"

"No." Larry gulped and licked his lips. "Work for Bar Sixteen. We're neighbors, just helping out neighbors. That's all. Honest."

"No rustlers here," Nantaje said.

"And I believe you!" He was sounding desperate.

Nantaje grabbed a pair of reins that someone had left draped over the side of the stall and tied the man's hands and feet together and left him lying there on his belly. There was a window without glass nearby, and Nantaje had just finished when he saw the second man approaching. The Apache found a rag from the corner of the stall and stuffed it into Larry's mouth. He clamped the knife between his teeth and scrambled swiftly up a rope into the hayloft overhead.

"Hey, Larry? Where are you? What you doing in there?" A wary note edged the man's voice.

Nantaje remained motionless in the loft, hearing footsteps halt just outside the barn door. Then a shadow moved across the dusty floor below and the crunch of dry straw beneath the man's boots rose faintly to Nantaje's keen ears.

"Larry?" He drew the name out into a long, slow question.

The shadow moved and a man stepped into view below. He advanced cautiously, the revolver in his hand in constant motion as his eyes probed worriedly into the dark corners and empty horse stalls. He came upon the stall where Nantaje had left the first man bound up.

"Larry!"

The fellow on the floor squirmed, trying to blurt out a warning.

He turned him over and worked the wadded rag from his mouth.

"There's an Injun in here!"

"What?"

"Look out!"

The warning came too late. Nantaje launched himself from the loft and drove the unsuspecting man to the floor. The impact stunned him, and the hilt of Nantaje's scalping knife knocked him out cold. With both men lashed to posts and gagged, he collected their firearms, then slipped soundlessly out the back door into the tall weeds and circled toward the cabin.

"Both have been gone for a long time," Louvel noted casually as he played a game of solitaire at the table.

Cadell was at the door, trying to keep an eye out for Larry and Frank while keeping Ridere and Louvel covered. He was getting nervous, and Louvel figured that just might be useful. He caught Ridere's eye and inclined his head at the crutch on the floor at their feet.

Ridere bent and took it up. Cadell seemed not to notice, or if he had, he saw nothing sinister in the action. At the same time Louvel gathered up the playing cards. Pinching the deck in his fingers, he aimed them at the window. When Cadell's attention was turned outside, Louvel gave them a squeeze and sent them cascading out of his hand. Like the flutter of a hundred bats' wings, they streamed across the little cabin and ricocheted off the window.

Cadell wheeled toward the window, startled.

Ridere leaped off the edge of the bed, and in spite of the pain in his leg he drove the end of the crutch into Cadell's gut. At the same instant something moved outside. By the time Ridere and Louvel made it out the door, Nantaje had the foreman of the Bar Sixteen pinned to the ground.

The Indian looked up and gave one of his rare grins. "For a while it looked like you expected me to take care of all three of them, Louvel."

The Southerner grinned. "An Apache's work is never done."

"Will you two get serious?" Ridere limped back inside and came out with a rope. They tied Cadell's hands and marched him down to the barn, where Nantaje had left his friends. They secured him with the others and Louvel bent over Cadell and shook his head. "Ah reckon there really was an Indian prowling about after all."

Cadell scowled back and yanked at the ropes tied to a stall post. "Jacob and his men will come looking for you."

"They won't have any trouble," Louvel assured him. "We will be in Mariposa Springs at the hanging."

"Not if we don't hurry up," Ridere urged. "We've already wasted too much time. We need to go now!"

Nantaje brought the horses around to the front of the barn. They saddled the animals and five minutes later had left the little cabin behind. But they still had a long ride to Mariposa Springs, and the sun was already high in the sky. Judging by where it stood, Louvel knew they were cutting it close. Too close. They could not afford another delay. Unlike a cat, Lionel only had one life to lose. There wasn't a whole lot of sand left in his hourglass.

Chapter Fourteen

How many times had he speculated on his own death; how it might come, or when? He hadn't pondered the event lately, but in the early days, he was certain it would be at the end of a whip in the hands of his overseer. Then later, when he'd made his break, by pursuing patrollers, or by an arrow in Indian Territory. In his later years, however, he figured he'd just get bucked off a bronc one day and never wake up. Not once had he ever imagined his last moments this side of eternity might be with a hangman's rope around his neck and a hundred gawking faces gathered around watching.

He paced his cell, fear crushing his chest like a giant's fist. Past the bars that protected the window stood the gray skeleton of the hangman's gallows. A man was testing it by dropping sacks of sand through the trapdoor. With each dull thud of the rope snapping taunt, Lionel's heart beat a little faster, his sweat flowed freer.

A desperate urge to escape suddenly overcame him and he flung himself against the bars, accomplishing nothing except to send a wave of pain into his arm and shoulder. It was hopeless. Lionel was a doomed man and he knew it.

The rattle of a key sent his heart climbing up into his throat. In the office the timber door squeaked open on its iron hinges. Sheriff Hodgeback, his deputy and John Jacob and Casey crowded inside. Hodgeback had a stubby scattergun in the crook of his arm, while Warren, the deputy, carried a pair of shackles.

Lionel's knuckles whitened around the iron bars. His view shot past the lawmen and found Jacob's unhappy face. Casey was frowning deeply too. Lionel knew that Casey had been made foreman since Driscoll's killing, but he'd not spoken to the man since before the trial.

The trial! It had all happened so fast, he could scarce believe it had only been four days ago that he'd found and helped that snakebit stranger. Was that snakebit stranger still holed up at his place? He knew he wasn't. Any sensible man would have hightailed it away from there first chance he got. Murder was a sticky web to get entangled in . . . especially if you were innocent. Best to flee it while you can. Lionel didn't blame Ridere for running. He'd likely have done the same had the boot been on the other foot.

"Time to go, Lionel," Hodgeback said. "Sure you don't want to have no final words with the parson before you take this walk?"

Lionel appeared not to hear him. His eyes were locked onto John Jacob's face. "Yo' know I didn't kill Driscoll." It was a final plea for help, help that Lionel knew no one could give him now.

Jacob glanced down and said softly, "I'm sorry,

Lionel. You don't know how sorry. But I . . . I got to go with the verdict."

Lionel's view shifted to Casey. Casey winced and gave a small shake of his head. It was final now. There'd be no last-minute reprieve. Lionel wasn't surprised.

"Time to go," the sheriff repeated. "Stand clear of the door." The key clicked in the lock.

Warren started in, but Lionel's eyes widened at the shackles and he said, "No not them. I swore I'd never be a shackled man again. Don't make me wear 'em. I won't wear 'em!"

"Are those really necessary?" Casey asked.

Hodgeback considered a moment, then nodded. "All right, I won't make you wear them, Lionel. I'll let you keep that much of your dignity intact. Only bear in mind, I'll be at your backside with this here scattergun sniffing your knees. You make a break for it, I cut those pins right out from under you. I'll do it in a heartbeat, and you will be dragged up the steps to keep your appointment with the hangman. That's a promise, and there ain't no dignity in dying that way, boy, so don't even think about making a break." Hodgeback nodded at Warren. The deputy retreated from the cell and drew his revolver to back up the sheriff's threat.

Hodgeback was right. There could be no dignity in running, and Lionel would not bring disgrace down upon himself. He stepped out of the cell, and as they closed in around him in the tight hallway, he stood straight and lifted his head. If this was to be his last walk, he *was* going to take it with dignity. That was all he had left.

John Russell Keane peered worriedly down the long street. Ridere said he'd be here. What could have happened to detain him? Had he changed his mind? He glanced at O'Brian. The Irishman was fidgeting, scratching at his cheek like he always did when he got nervous.

"Where in blazes are they?" O'Brian said.

"Ridere better get here soon." They were standing on the boardwalk with maybe forty other people who had begun to gather on this gloomy morning for the hanging. Through a storefront window, Keane watched the hands of a wall clock creep toward the eleven o'clock hour.

"Maybe he changed his mind."

Keane shook his head. "Louvel wouldn't let him."

Nearby, the wranglers from the Lazy J were milling about. Some had stopped off at the saloon to fortify themselves for the coming execution. In the family carriage, Felicity and Rachel sat beneath the canvas roof while the farrier, Harvey Oldebrook, held the horses. Both the women wore frowns and pretended as if the other was not there. At one point Felicity bent and whispered something in her daughter's ear, but Rachel remained unmoving and might have easily passed for a plaster mannequin.

Riders came into town from the south and tied up in front of the General Mercantile. The hanging was drawing in the curious from all the outlying ranches. Keane grimaced. *Where was Ridere?* He strode out into the street with the other men and women and worked his way to the side of the carriage. The girl didn't smile.

"How is that ankle feeling today, Miss Jacob?" Keane asked.

"It hurts, but not too bad," she replied briefly.

"The swelling is starting to go down," Felicity added, sounding more optimistic than her daughter, or at least trying to. There was not much to be optimistic about today, especially if Ridere didn't get there soon.

"There he is," Rachel said, the words catching in her throat.

The sheriff and her father emerged from the jailhouse with Lionel in front of them. The deputy and Casey Owen walked nearby. Blake discovered Keane by the carriage just then and looked startled. He covered it up quickly and came through the crowd.

"You okay, Rachel?" he asked. His eyes were fixed upon Keane.

"I'm all right," she replied sharply, as if she was getting weary of people inquiring after her well-being.

As they escorted Lionel across the street toward the gallows, John Jacob kept searching the crowd, as if looking for someone. His view swept past the carriage and momentarily lingered there. Keane saw the frown deepen on the ranch owner's face, then his searching eyes moved on.

Keane knew now that Ridere was not going to make it in time. Ridere had been Lionel's last hope, and now that hope had evaporated. "That man is innocent," Keane said softly, and only Blake, Felicity and Rachel heard him.

"Not according to the witnesses and the jury," Blake countered quickly. "He's guilty all right. Everyone knows he killed Driscoll."

"Everyone?" Keane leveled a cool eye at Blake and said, "Not everyone. You know he didn't do it." The certainty in his voice made Blake's jaw tighten and the veins down his neck stand out like the cords of a lariat.

"You don't know what you're talking about."

"I know an innocent man is about to die, and I know the real killer is here in this crowd right now. And you know it too."

He heard the sharp intake of a breath, and when he

looked up, Felicity's eyes had rounded and were staring at him.

"Isn't that right, Mrs. Jacob? Driscoll was killed by someone who had a real good motive. Someone driven by love, and maybe fear?"

"Shut up," Blake hissed.

By this time the men had marched Lionel to the gallows and had stopped at the steps that climbed to the platform. The crowd quieted down. Rachel fidgeted on the carriage seat, her glances shifting between Felicity and Blake.

Blake gave her his hand to squeeze and she looked across the crowd at her father.

John Jacob's fists were clenching and unclenching at his sides. He glanced at Keane and stiffened like a dead man.

The hangman took Lionel by the arm. The black man balked at the first step. Hodgeback prodded him on with his scattergun, and the three of them started up. The thirteen steps might have been ten feet high each for all the effort it took Lionel to climb them. He looked out over the crowd but refused to cry out his innocence now.

Keane glanced at Felicity.

"What?" she asked, startled.

"How far are you going to let this go?"

"I don't know what you are talking about," she said, her breathing coming in quick pants now.

"How about it, Blake? You going to stand there and let it happen?"

The young man glared at him.

Keane nodded toward John Jacob. "He's going to let them go through with it. He's going to let them hang that man."

Rachel said to Keane, "What are you trying to do to us?"

"What am I trying to do?" Keane asked. "Only what any man would do. What I did at the Salt River to protect the lives of all those Apache women and children. What I would do again out of honor . . . out of justice. If I didn't try to stop this now, it would weigh heavy upon my spirit all the rest of my life."

Rachel looked away from him, staring at the gallows. Lionel was standing on the trap door. Hodgeback had tied the black man's hands.

"He's all out of time," Keane said, considering each of them. "Honor or disgrace. Without honor, what is left?"

Blake's face blanched. He knew it was true. Keane could see it in Rachel's eyes as well. Felicity's face was frozen in fear. Keane turned away from them.

"You got any last words you want to say, Lionel?" the sheriff asked.

Lionel peered at the crowd that had gathered in town. His view found John Jacob, and the two men stared at each other until Jacob could take it no longer and looked away.

"I got nothing to say to no one." He held his head up and threw his shoulders back as the hangman slipped the black hood over his head. After adjusting the noose about Lionel's neck, the hangman made his way down the steps. Only Hodgeback and Lionel remained on the gallows. There was a long moment of silence. Keane knew Lionel would be doing more suffering in these final few seconds than at the end of that last neck-snapping fall.

He looked at Rachel. The girl seemed on the edge of saying something. "Honor or disgrace?" he asked, wondering if she was remembering the talk they'd had the day before. Keane knew he had a decision to make too, and the time for waiting was past.

The hangman went around the side of the gallows and stopped near the lever. John Jacob was standing alongside it and stepped back as the man reached for the lever that would send Lionel on his way to eternity.

Rachel stood in the carriage and shouted, "Stop!"

John Jacob's expression went wide. Her exclamation had shaped his face with fear. "Don't say anything!" he ordered.

"He didn't do it," she shouted. Her words stirred the crowd, and a murmur arose among the people. "I know who did!"

"Rachel!" John Jacob was near panic. "Lionel done it. We all know it. He's guilty!" he said, looking around the crowd. "Pull the lever!"

Like the rest of them, the hangman had been stunned by her declaration. He stood there, uncertain now of the proper way to proceed. He glanced at Hodgeback, looking for the answer.

"I said pull that lever!" Jacob raged, but the hangman wasn't about to until Hodgeback gave the nod, and the sheriff, still sorting out the implications of Rachel's statement, wasn't giving one.

"Then I'll do it!" Jacob lunged past the hangman before anyone could stop him and grabbed for the lever.

A rifle shot came from up the street. The bullet splintered the wood beneath Jacob's hand and he jerked the hand back. Ridere, Louvel and Nantaje rode into the crowd and drew up. Ridere levered a fresh round into the chamber and said, "This man is innocent. I was there and saw how it happened."

Keane had been a heartbeat away from intervening in the hanging himself. Now he let it go and caught

O'Brian's eye. The Irishman was standing near the gallows just in case he was needed. But it was Ridere who, in the end, had stopped John Jacob from carrying out his own brand of justice.

The murmuring among the people swelled into a demand for an explanation. Up on the gallows, Hodgeback regained his composure.

"Everyone just settle down." He leveled his scattergun at Ridere, but the crowd was so thick in his direction he dare not use it. "Just who the devil are you, mister? Someone better do some talking real quick!" Then his view narrowed and his voice was suddenly wary. "Don't I know you from somewhere?"

Ridere said, "I was in Lionel's cabin the evening Egan Driscoll was murdered. I saw everything through the window. Lionel didn't shoot that man. The shot came from down by the creek that runs past his place."

"If what you say is true, why didn't you come forward before now?"

Keane heard hesitation in Ridere's voice. "I got myself bit real bad by a rattlesnake, Sheriff. I tried to stop those men who took Lionel away, but I was too sick to make the door. Fell and knocked myself out cold on the edge of a chair. Only now feeling well enough to ride."

That wasn't exactly true. Ridere had conveniently left out the part about being afraid to face Hodgeback, that being the real reason he hadn't come forward sooner. But Keane figured it a moot point now.

"All right mister, suppose you tell me who did the killing then?"

"I don't know that. The killer was down among the trees. All I saw was the muzzle flash from the rifle. That was when Lionel grabbed up his own rifle, to defend himself. And the next moment those other men came rushing up from the barn. They saw Lionel holding his rifle and Driscoll shot dead."

"So, who did kill Driscoll? Seems like all I got is the word of a stranger."

Keane knew the time had come for him to speak up. "There is someone else here who knows what happened. Several, in fact."

"And who might you be?"

"My name is John Russell Keane."

Hodgeback scowled as he searched his memory. "I remember you, and you . . . and you," he said, his view skipping from Louvel to Nantaje, lingering a moment upon the Apache. "We met on the road a few days ago."

"That's right. Since that time I've been working on the Lazy J, and I've learned a few things about the murder."

Rachel glanced at her mother, then Blake and finally at the terror that consumed her father's face. "I'll tell," she said weakly, turning her sad eyes back at Blake.

"Don't, Rachel, don't tell them anything!" Blake said, panic rising in his voice. He looked from her to Keane, and then spied the Winchester under the carriage seat and snatched it up.

"What are you doing?" Rachel screamed.

Blake levered a shell and the crowd gave way before the muzzle of the gun. "All right, I admit it. I killed Driscoll. It was me and no one else."

"What are you saying, Peter?" Rachel cried.

"I know what I'm doing."

Keane started around the carriage, but Blake leveled the rifle at him. "I knew you were trouble right from the start. Kept putting your nose where it didn't belong."

"Put the rifle down, Blake. There has been enough heartache come out of Driscoll's death. No need to add any more to it."

"Shut up and stay back!" Blake raised his voice so all the people there could hear him. "I done it and nobody is gonna take the blame for it anymore." Blake bolted for a horse tied nearby.

"Stop that man!" Hodgeback ordered.

Blake swung toward the gallows and squeezed off a shot at the sheriff. Hodgeback flinched and ducked around a post. He came back around and the shotgun in his fist roared.

In the street, Blake lurched and hit the ground hard . . . and didn't move.

Chapter Fifteen

"Peter!"

Rachel scrambled out of the carriage and rushed to where he had fallen, dropping at his side. With a crowd gathering around, she turned him over, then stared at the blood on her hands. Blake's eyes opened at her touch; glazed and unfocused, they searched, then found her face.

"Don't cry," he said, feebly lifting a hand and touching the line of moisture down her cheek. She grabbed his fingers and squeezed them tight.

Someone in the crowd called for a doctor, but Keane had seen plenty of wounded men in the army, and he knew Blake was dying.

"I did it," he said softly, his view fixed upon her face. "No one else is to blame. Lionel is innocent." He looked at the people there. "Did you hear me? I done it," he said harshly. The effort drained the last of his strength.

Rachel began to weep bitterly. Hodgeback came through the crowd with Jacob and Casey at his side. Blake looked up at the sheriff and swallowed hard. "You know now?" he breathed, failing.

"I know," Hodgeback said. "Why'd you make me do it, kid? Why did you make me have to shoot you?"

"Somebody . . . had . . . to pay," Blake managed. His breath drained away, a shudder ran through him and pale eyes rolled up into his head.

Rachel knelt there crying, her mother and father near. Sheriff Hodgeback slowly shook his head.

When Ridere and the others rode over, Keane said, "Took your time getting here, didn't you, Harry?"

Louvel said, "Mr. Jacob sent some men to the cabin to keep us there. Claimed we were rustling his cows."

"Did he now?" Keane glanced at Jacob and got a hard, stormy look from the man in return.

"Why did the kid do it?" Hodgeback wondered, regret in his voice. "Why did he break and run like that? Why'd he make me kill him?"

Casey stirred himself from his shock and said, "At least you didn't hang an innocent man, Sheriff. That would have been worse."

"Yep, that would have been a bad thing," he admitted. "Least now it's all over with. We got the killer and he paid the price."

"That is not true, Sheriff," Keane said.

"I don't want to hear any more from you!" John Jacob barked, glaring at Keane.

Keane gave him a tight grin. "I don't find that too surprising, Mr. Jacob, considering . . ."

Jacob stiffened, the dread returning to his face.

"What do you mean?" Hodgeback demanded.

"Letting Blake take the blame for Driscoll's murder is exactly what Jacob was hoping for. Oh, he didn't have Blake in mind for it right at the beginning. Lionel was the scapegoat, and that suited his purposes just fine, isn't that right?" Keane held the portly owner of the Lazy J in his steady glare.

"I don't know what you are talking about!" But it was plain Jacob had been shaken by the accusation.

Keane stuck a hand into his pocket and came out with the brass cartridges. "These came from the gun that killed Driscoll. The same gun was used to ambush me a few days later. They're thirty-eights."

"What does that prove?" Jacob asked sharply.

Keane bent for the Winchester and dragged it out from under Blake's body. "This gun belongs to you, doesn't it?"

"It's mine," Jacob admitted "So what?

"It's a thirty-eight. The same gun that killed Driscoll."

"Kinda hard to prove that, ain't it, mister?" Hodgeback said.

Keane worked the lever, catching the spent cartridge that flipped from the breech. "If you check, you'll see that this cartridge and those match. There is a mark of the bolt face of this rifle that exactly matches the one left on the heads of those cartridges."

Hodgeback studied them for a moment, then slowly swiveled an eye at Jacob. "He's right."

"John!" Felicity exclaimed. "Not you? How could you?"

Jacob had begun to sweat. His startled eyes leaped from his wife to the wide stare of his daughter. Then something changed in his eyes. They grew suddenly cool and calculating. "You know why, Felicity," he told his wife. "Need I announce it to the world so that everyone in town knows?"

Keane caught a wince come to Hodgeback's face. It

passed in an instant and the sheriff said, "I don't understand all of this, but it looks like I'm going to have to lock you up, John. At least until I sort through all that has happened." He was considering Blake's body with a puzzled look on his face. "Got two men who claimed to have murdered Driscoll." He shook his head. "Two of you couldn't have done it."

"They both lied to you, Sheriff," Keane said.

Hodgeback's head snapped around. "But you just said it was Jacob who done it?"

"No, I only said it was his rifle that killed Driscoll, and ambushed me. But you see, the murderer rode a horse with a narrow hoof, and that horse belongs to Casey Owen."

"Casey!" Jacob exclaimed looking at his foreman. "Of course! You wanted Driscoll's job, and you knew where I kept that rifle. And you've been with me so long, no one would have thought anything of you coming into my office to take it. They'd just think you were about ranch business."

Casey was stunned by the accusation and backed up a step, but some of the townsmen crowded close and stopped him.

"No, you got it all wrong," Casey said. "I had no use for Driscoll, but I'd never murder the man!"

Hodgeback was beside himself. "Wait up now, everyone! Somebody done the killing, and it can't be that Casey, Jacob and Blake all pulled the trigger together!"

"And they didn't, did they, Mrs. Jacob?" Keane said, shifting his view to her startled face. "In fact none of them murdered Driscoll, did they, Mrs. Jacob? And that leaves the one who is the real murderer." He was looking only at her now. "Why is it you suddenly decided to leave the ranch and go back east?"

"You know perfectly well why she wants to leave," Rachel said in her mother's defense. "Please don't bring it up here," she implored, looking at the townspeople standing around.

"Yes, I know. What I didn't know was why she was so anxious to take you along, especially since neither you nor your father wanted it to happen. Then it occurred to me. There could be only one reason, but I couldn't be certain until I talked with Harvey Oldebrook and he told me that Casey's horse was something special to him, and that he let no one else ride it. In fact, he keeps it with the horses in the barn, doesn't he? But the pieces only came together after you ran away yesterday afternoon, Miss Jacob. Seems that since your horse was recovering from a hurt leg, you were in the habit of taking any horse you could get your hands on. That night when Driscoll was killed, it was Casey's horse you took, wasn't it, Miss Jacob?"

"That's a lie!" John Jacob roared.

Rachel shook her head. "No, Father, it's not. It is time for all the lying to stop, for all the killing to stop." She placed a hand gently on Blake's lifeless chest and sobbed bitterly.

When she finally sniffed and wiped her eyes dry she stood and faced Hodgeback. "I killed Egan Driscoll. I took Father's rifle and Casey's horse, and I did it."

Felicity drew Rachel to her chest and hugged her suffocatingly tight.

Fear pulled at her father's face, while Hodgeback stood there looking more confused than before.

Keane handed Hodgeback the rifle and said, "Egan Driscoll took delight in tormenting the people around him. He rode Blake constantly, belittling him in front of her and anyone else. And Rachel was not immune to his poison either, in spite of the fact that she was the daughter of his boss"—Keane lowered his voice until only Hodgeback could hear—"and of his lover."

Hodgeback's eyes widened and moved toward Felicity.

"But *we* don't want to go down that road, now do *we*, Sheriff? Not in front of all these people." Keane glanced at Ridere, then back at the sheriff. At that moment Hodgeback must have remembered where he'd seen Ridere before, and he understood Keane's warning too.

"No, we don't need to go there," he said. He looked at Blake, then Jacob. "They were both willing to lie to save her from the crime she done."

"If you were her father, wouldn't you be willing to take your daughter's place at the end of a hangman's rope?" Keane asked. "Felicity knew the truth too. She was willing to take her daughter far away from here to protect her."

"And Blake's reason?"

"That should be plain enough for anyone with two eyes and even the vaguest memory of when they were young and smitten for the first time."

"What about you being ambushed? She do that too?"

"No. Blake suspected I was getting too close to the truth. But he only wanted to scare me off, not kill me. You see, Rachel confessed to him what she had done. It was eating her up inside and she had to confide in someone she trusted. That was when he decided to take matters into his own hands. If he'd meant to kill me, he easily could have. But you see, Blake wasn't a murderer."

Rachel pushed herself from her mother's arms and turned toward the sheriff. "I'm sorry I led everyone on. I'm sorry I nearly let Lionel die for my crime." She looked at the tall black man still standing upon the gallows. The noose was no longer around his neck, nor the hood over his eyes. The hangman was standing there with him.

"Untie that man and let him go," Hodgeback ordered. He came around and faced Rachel. "I don't really know what to do with you, miss. I reckon that's for a judge and jury to decide."

"Judge Canaby?" she asked.

"Yep."

Jacob moaned. "Oh, no. Good Lord no. Not Canaby."

Hodgeback took Rachel by the arm and started her toward the jail. But she turned suddenly and looked up into Keane's face.

"Why? Why did Peter do it, Mr. Keane?"

Keane didn't know if he had a good answer to that, but he tried. "Remember that night when you asked me why some people do what they did?"

"I was speaking of myself."

"I see that now."

"You said they did things out of their wants or out of their needs. Out of disgrace or out of honor." She looked puzzled. "I still don't understand."

"That's because I left one out."

"Which one?" she asked.

"I left out the most important one of all. Love. Blake did what he thought he had to do to save you, Rachel. Because he loved you."

Her eyes welled again, and she looked down at the body at her feet. The sheriff walked her across the street and into the jailhouse.

John Jacob was barely holding back his tears. Felicity hesitated, then stood beside him and folded an arm around his waist.

Keane grimaced and knew their pain. He'd seen it in

the eyes of wives and children whose loved ones failed to return after a patrol or a battle. He'd seen it in the faces of the Apache too. But thinking of the injustice nearly accomplished here, a lump began to form in his gut, and it turned to a hard stone just sitting there.

"I wouldn't worry about Judge Canaby too much," he told them.

Jacob glared at Keane. "How can you say that? You show up out of nowhere, force yourself into our lives and now my daughter is in jail! Canaby's a hard man, a man who doesn't balk at seeing justice done." John Jacob seethed with anger.

"I know he is a hard man," Keane said, thinking over all that had happened. "But looks to me like there's two sorts of justice in this town."

"What do you mean?"

"You should know. Harvey told me all about it. There is white justice, and then there is black justice." Keane watched Lionel descending the gallow's stairs.

"I suspect Rachel will be getting some of the former from Canaby."

"When de chips was down, Mr. John and his family was all willing to throw me to de wolves." Lionel shook his head. "Makes a man feel like he ain't worth much, don't it, Mr. Harry?"

"I don't understand it," Ridere said.

"Maybe someday, when you have kids, Harry, and they go wrong, you will," Keane remarked.

"Maybe."

"It still doesn't make it right," Louvel noted.

"Never said it did. Only that he would understand."

Keane, Louvel, O'Brian, Ridere and Nantaje were together outside the hotel, their horses saddled and packed. Although Mariposa Springs started out a pleasant enough place, they were all anxious to be away from there. Especially Ridere, who did not trust Sheriff Hodgeback, in spite of the unspoken threat of revealing his own wife's indiscretions that Keane had left with him.

"What are you going to do now?" Keane asked Lionel.

The sky was still gray and threatening to spit rain any minute. It was late in the day, but the town was still full of the people who'd come in for the hanging. They seemed to have acquired a morbid curiosity about the intended guest of honor of that necktie party. Their open stares and whispered words jangled Lionel's nerves almost as much as the feel of the rope around his neck had.

"One thing for sure, I can't go back to working for Mr. John, even if he would take me back." Lionel looked around the town and said, "This place has got de feel of a cold and clammy shirt. I figure de only thing left for me to do is move on."

"Ever consider California?" Keane asked.

"What's in California?"

"San Francisco," Louvel said.

"*Señoritas*," O'Brian answered with a leering grin tilted toward Ridere.

"I . . . I don't know anymore," Ridere admitted.

O'Brian chuckled. "Once burned, twice shy. You'll get over it, Harry."

"The Pacific Ocean," Nanatje allowed.

Lionel considered the offer with frowning eyes and a thoughtful pucker to his lips. "But what's der for me?"

"That's something every man has to decide for himself, I reckon," Keane said. "But if you've got a hankering to move on, you're welcome to ride with us."

"You all feel dat way?"

They said they did—all except Royden Louvel, who had to give the matter some thought. After a moment he said in his soft Southern drawl, "Ah suppose if Ah can get used to riding with a damn Yankee, Ah can ride with just about anyone, even a runaway."

Keane grinned. "Coming from Captain Louvel, that's practically an engraved invitation, Lionel."

"I'd have to go back to my cabin for some things."

"I reckon California can wait that long," Keane said, shoving a boot into the stirrup and swinging up onto his horse.

⊕UTCASTS

THE OUTCAST BRIGADE

JASON ELDER

They are not wanted where they come from. They are not welcome anywhere. They are outcasts, rootless and friendless, until luck or destiny throw them together. A former Apache scout shunned by his tribe, an ex-Union Army major, a former Confederate captain, and two army deserters, all forced to band together to stay alive—as long as they can avoid killing each other. Can they bury their anger and work together long enough to do what they have to do? Can they make it to Mexico to rescue a band of friendly Apaches who have been captured and sold into slavery? It is no easy task, because even if they manage not to kill each other, there are plenty of others eager to do it for them.

___4699-7 $3.99 US/$4.99 CAN

BRANDISH

DOUGLAS HIRT

FIRST TIME IN PAPERBACK!

Captain Ethan Brandish has finally given up his command of Fort Lowell, deep in Apache territory. But the vicious Apache leader, Yellow Shirt, has another fate in store for him. He and a group of renegade warriors attack a stage station and ride off just before Brandish arrives. But the Apaches are still out there—watching and waiting—and Brandish must risk his own life to save the few wounded survivors.

___4323-8 $4.50 US/$5.50 CAN

WILL HENRY

CHIRICAHUA

"Some of the best writing the American West can claim!"
—Brian Garfield, Bestselling Author of
Death Wish

Led by the dreaded Geronimo and Chatto, a band of Chiricahua Apache warriors sweep up out of Mexico in a red deathwind. Their vow—to destroy every white life in their bloody path across the Arizona Territory. But between the swirling forces of white and red hatred, history sends a lone Indian rider named Pa-nayo-tishn, The Coyote Saw Him, crying peace—and the fate of the Chiricahuas and all free Apaches is altered forever.

The Spur Award–winning Novel of the West
___4266-5 $4.50 US/$5.50

Dorchester Publishing Co., Inc.
P.O. Box 6640
Wayne, PA 19087-8640

Please add $1.75 for shipping and handling for the first book and $.50 for each book thereafter. NY, NYC, and PA residents, please add appropriate sales tax. No cash, stamps, or C.O.D.s. All orders shipped within 6 weeks via postal service book rate. Canadian orders require $2.00 extra postage and must be paid in U.S. dollars through a U.S. banking facility.

Name_____
Address_____
City_____State_____Zip_____
I have enclosed $_____ in payment for the checked book(s).
Payment <u>must</u> accompany all orders. ☐ Please send a free catalog.

THE LAST WARPATH

"The most critically acclaimed Western writer of this or any other time!"
—Loren D. Estleman

The battle between the U.S. Cavalry and the wild-riding Cheyenne, lords of the North Prairie, rages across the Western plains for forty years. The white man demands peace or total war, and the Cheyenne will not pay the price of peace. Great leaders like Little Wolf and Dull Knife know their people are meant to range with the eagle and the wolf. The mighty Cheyenne will fight to be free until the last warrior has gone forever upon the last warpath.

FIVE-TIME WINNER OF THE
GOLDEN SPUR AWARD

___4314-9 $4.50 US/$5.50 CAN
Dorchester Publishing Co., Inc.
P.O. Box 6640
Wayne, PA 19087-8640

Please add $1.75 for shipping and handling for the first book and $.50 for each book thereafter. NY, NYC, and PA residents, please add appropriate sales tax. No cash, stamps, or C.O.D.s. All orders shipped within 6 weeks via postal service book rate. Canadian orders require $2.00 extra postage and must be paid in U.S. dollars through a U.S. banking facility.

Name_____
Address_____
City_____State_____Zip
I have enclosed $_____ in payment for the checked book(s).
Payment <u>must</u> accompany all orders. ❑ Please send a free catalog.

YELLOWSTONE KELLY

Yellowstone Kelly is an Indian fighter and scout like no other. The devil-may-care Irishman can pick off hostiles and quote the classics with equal ease and accuracy. Even the mighty Sioux fear him. Most of them. Sitting Bull's main war chief, the dreaded Gall, fears no man, and Kelly has something of his that the warrior will gladly kill to get back—his woman.

___4364-5 $4.99 US/$5.99 CAN

Dorchester Publishing Co., Inc.
P.O. Box 6640
Wayne, PA 19087-8640

Please add $1.75 for shipping and handling for the first book and $.50 for each book thereafter. NY, NYC, and PA residents, please add appropriate sales tax. No cash, stamps, or C.O.D.s. All orders shipped within 6 weeks via postal service book rate. Canadian orders require $2.00 extra postage and must be paid in U.S. dollars through a U.S. banking facility.

Name_____

Address_____

City_____State_____Zip_____

I have enclosed $_____ in payment for the checked book(s).

Payment <u>must</u> accompany all orders. ☐ Please send a free catalog.

WILL HENRY

WHO RIDES WITH WYATT

"Some of the best writing the American West can claim!"
—Brian Garfield, Bestselling Author of Death Wish

They call Tombstone the Sodom in the Sagebrush. It is a town of smoking guns and raw guts, stage stick-ups and cattle runoffs, blazing shotguns and men bleeding in the streets. Then Wyatt Earp comes to town and pins on a badge. Before he leaves Tombstone, the lean, tall man with ice-blue eyes, a thick mustache and a long-barreled Colt becomes a legend, the greatest gunfighter of all time.

BY THE FIVE-TIME WINNER OF THE GOLDEN SPUR AWARD

____4292-4 $3.99 US/$4.99 CAN

UNDER THE BURNING SUN

H. A. DeRosso

Of all the amazing writers published in the popular fiction magazines of the 1940s and '50s, one of the greatest was H.A. DeRosso. Within twenty years he published nearly two hundred Western short stories, all noted for their brilliant style, their realism and their compelling vision of the dark side of the Old West. Now, finally, for the first time in paperback, we have a collection of the best work of this true master of the Western story. This collection, edited by Bill Pronzini, presents a cross-section of DeRosso's Western fiction, spanning his entire career. Here are eleven of his best stories and his riveting short novel, "The Bounty Hunter," all powerful and spellbinding, and all filled with the excitement, the passion, and the poetry of Western writing at its peak.

___4712-8 $4.50 US/$5.50 CAN

Dorchester Publishing Co., Inc.
P.O. Box 6640
Wayne, PA 19087-8640

Please add $1.75 for shipping and handling for the first book and $.50 for each book thereafter. NY, NYC, and PA residents, please add appropriate sales tax. No cash, stamps, or C.O.D.s. All orders shipped within 6 weeks via postal service book rate. Canadian orders require $2.00 extra postage and must be paid in U.S. dollars through a U.S. banking facility.

Name_____
Address_____
City_____ State_____ Zip_____
I have enclosed $ _____ in payment for the checked book(s).
Payment <u>must</u> accompany all orders. ❑ Please send a free catalog.

WILD BILL

JUDD COLE

SANTA FE DEATH TRAP

All Wild Bill Hickok wants as he sets out for Santa Fe is a place to lie low for a while, to get away from the fame and notoriety that follows him wherever he goes. But fame isn't the only thing that sticks to Wild Bill like glue. He made a lot of enemies over the years. And one of them, Frank Tutt, has waited a good long time to taste sweet revenge. He knows Wild Bill is on his way to Santa Fe and he is ready for him . . . ready and eager to make him pay. But after all these years he can wait a bit longer, long enough to play a little game with his legendary target. Oh, he will kill Wild Bill, all right—but first he wants Bill to know what it is like to live in Hell.

___4720-9 $3.99 US/$4.99 CAN